Also by Clay Cassidy

Payback
The Judge
The Return
The Serial Killer
A Dozen Lawmen
Wrong Diagnosis
Rebel Cowgirl

Table of Contents

Rebel Cowgirl
Clay Cassidy

Edited and Published by Clay Cassidy

Dedication

I dedicate this novel to my beloved granddaughter. She is an avid reader and loves to read books of any genre. She is bound to reach great heights.

Prologue

Five years previously; dusk, some-where in West Texas.

The horse that enters the larger-than-average town has lost its spunk; almost dragging its body on hooves that are short of three ironclad shoes. A figure resembling that of a young female, struggles to keep herself in the saddle while holding onto the pommel to do so.

What catches the eyes are the twin low-slung six-shooters riding her hips on either side. A second glance at the girl will leave a man astonished at her beauty, something not noticeable at first glance. Her clothes are trail-worn and dirty; dust and sweat mingling to form a thin-layered crust on her skin.

Reaching the Livery, the girl sits astride her mount for a moment before dismounting. The Liveryman stands idly by and waits. He sees that the figure has difficulty in standing alone and tries to lend a helping hand. Cautiously taking hold of the rider's arm, he speaks in a gentle manner.

"You alright, mister? Pardon me for sayin' so, but you look like shit. You want me te take care o' your hoss for you? I'd be glad to help ye get te the Hotel. We can talk about payin' me for your hoss tomorrow; when you feel better."

The figure reacts suddenly and without warning, exploding into a ball of fiery fury and shakes off the hand that holds its arm.

"I'm no mister, you idiot! If you call me that again, I'll pump you so full of lead your coffin'll be too heavy to carry! Just take care of my mount; I'm alright. I'll square up with you tomorrow for a stable and food for my horse."

CHAPTER ONE

Crystal Springs; late afternoon.

Logan Prescott stands outside the saloon on the boardwalk and looks into the crowded, smoke filled room. It seems that the entire town's men are gathered in this little room.

Logan is tall; reaching six foot one without his boots. His tall frame accentuates the well-formed wide shoulders and muscular arms. A tight six-pack ripples on his stomach. Logan's face is ruggedly handsome, yet boyishly young. On either side of a straight aristocratic nose, two green-blue eyes peer back from above a friendly mouth. Thick corn-blond hair brushes against his shirt collar.

Satisfied that he will be able to squeeze in, Logan pushes the batwing doors apart and whisks inside, making his way to the bar counter. Greetings reach Logan above the noise buzzing in his ears.

"Logan, how you doin', man? Haven't seen you in a long time! Come join us over here; we have a lot to talk about."

There are too many to mention by name, so Logan just raises his hand and returns each ones greeting in one swift motion of his hand, smiling as he does so.

"Howdy there, boys! Be with you in a short while."

Logan finds a spot at the bar counter and waits patiently for the barman to serve him.

"What'll it be, Logan; same as always?"

"Yeah, Whisky's fine, thanks Charlie."

Charlie Evans knows what just about all his regular customers drink. Logan doesn't frequent the bar often, but when he does, he only has Whisky. Anyway, he's always been a very mild drinker and never becomes intoxicated. He'll drink one, maybe two drinks and be on his way.

Everyone who lives in the surrounding area is fond of Logan. He is already in conversation with a couple of cowhands from one of the ranches. Accepting his drink with a nod and a smile from Charlie, Logan excuses himself from the bar and walks to the back, where he finds an empty table.

Pulling out the chair, Logan seats himself and leans back in it, taking in the scene around him. He is happy keeping to himself, just watching the other folk go about their business.

Logan takes his time finishing the drink before ordering another. He enjoys the strong, tangy flavor of the Whisky. With his drinks finished, Logan pushes his chair back and gets up. He leaves the money for his drinks on the table and puts his Stetson on, ready to leave the saloon.

Halfway across the floor towards the exit, there is a commotion outside. Suddenly one of the older citizens of the town breaks through the saloon doors with such force that one side breaks off its hinges. It's old Frank, the town drunk.

Logan watches in alarm as the beat-up figure tries to raise himself off the floor, and fails in his attempt. Then everything becomes clear as another familiar figure enters the saloon. The man is the same age as Logan, but not as imposing.

Logan walks to where old Frank is lying. Taking him by his hand and lifting him off the ground by his elbow, Logan helps him off the floor and sits him in a chair. He turns around, facing the other man. The other man is visibly agitated and it sounds in his voice when he speaks.

"What the hell you do that for, Prescott? You shouldn't stick your nose where it don't belong! Did'n your daddy ever teach you that? Now bring Frank back an' put him where he was; I ain't done with him yet!"

Logan stares unblinkingly at the figure facing him, his gaze not shifting from that of the other man. Sam Cohen is a good two inches shorter than Logan is, with long untidy light-brown hair and bearded features. Grey eyes stare back, separated by a nose that has been broken several times before. Sam is of medium build.

"Well, Cohen, to start off with, as you opened the door for insults; your daddy ain't never been around, so if I were you, I wouldn't elaborate further on that issue. Now, to answer your first question; I happen to like Frank even though he's homeless and drinks a lot. Secondly, because of that exact same reason, it doesn't give you any right to treat him like dirt. Now, if you want Frank, you're going to have to go through me to get to him."

Three of Sam Cohen's ranch hands are with him. They look from Sam to Logan and back at Sam, not understanding why Sam doesn't say anything. To the three ranch hands, it's as clear as daylight what Sam has to do. They step forward threateningly, their hands resting on their gun butts.

Sam Cohen on the other hand, didn't expect Logan to stand in his way and protect Frank. Sam never considered the possibility that Logan would be at the saloon. He stares at the latter, then shrugs and waves his ranch hands down.

"Take it easy, boys. Have it your way, Logan. There's plenty of time to finish this little incident in my own time. Waste your time on that no-good piece of trash. Believe me when I tell you old Frank'll just as soon stab you in the back."

Logan looks at Frank where he sits on the chair, cradling his head between his hands. His nose is still bleeding, and droplets of blood fall on the table. Logan turns his gaze back to Sam, shaking his head.

"I don't think so, Sam. Frank's never done anybody any harm. You must've done something. Why'd you beat him like this?"

"He went for my gun! Damn well nearly succeeded too! He woulda shot me if I hadn't beaten the daylights out of him. I don't ..."

"Cut the bullshit, Sam! You're always busy conniving and cheating. Like I said, you must've done something to provoke him to act like he did. Maybe he was protecting himself. It don't matter; you won't get close enough to him again, anyway. You've always preyed on the weak, so this incident doesn't come as a surprise. I'm also warning you, Sam; don't let me catch you or any of your men near Frank here. You'll have me to reckon with, and I won't be playin' no games with you."

Sam's intense dislike for Logan mirrors in his eyes as they stare at each other.

Logan turns back to Frank and helps him to his feet. He uses his arm around Frank's waist in order to support the latter. They pass Sam and his three goons and walk out onto the boardwalk. Logan helps Frank to mount his horse, and leads it by the reins up the street to where the Doctor's rooms are.

It takes a while for Doctor Ford to examine old Frank, but he has a thorough report for Logan when he returns.

"Logan, old Frank took a pretty severe beating. He has some broken ribs, fractured right forearm, and broken bones in his face, including his nose. His jawbone is also broken in two places, and he's missing a few teeth. Frank has a slight concussion, and he'll have to rest for at least a week before he can even think of getting out of bed. I suggest that he stays here, where I can keep an eye on him and medicate him properly."

"Thanks, Doc; that'll do just fine. Keep him here and treat him. I'll pay you up front for the week. How much is it for the week's stay including the medication and cast for his arm?"

Doctor Ford treads around uneasy.

"You don't have to ..."

"Doc, I brought him here, so I'll pay for your services. How much?"

"Well, if you insist, Logan. It'll be sixty dollars for everything. He'll be in much better condition by Friday next week."

"Thanks again, doc. Don't allow Sam Cohen or any of his ranch hands to visit Frank while he's here. They're the reason he's lyin' in that bed here. I'll look in from time to time to find out how he's doin'. Take this; there's one hundred dollars. Use the extra money for whatever's necessary."

Logan heads in the direction of the Livery in town. He has decided to book a room for himself for the week it will take Frank to recuperate enough to travel.

He pays the young stable assistant at the Livery to ride out to his ranch, the Double L-Circle, and inform his foreman that he is staying in town for the week. It will cause a little inconvenience for Lucy though, seeing that they have arranged a get together for Friday evening with her parents at their ranch.

The get together would have been the perfect opportunity for Logan and Lucy to discuss their plans with her parents for their upcoming engagement.

SAM COHEN TURNS AROUND and faces his ranch hands. The expressions on their faces show that they aren't impressed with the way their employer has handled the situation with Logan. One of the ranchmen, a burly man in his late thirties, speaks on behalf of all of them.

"Why you let Prescott talk to you like that, Sam? We woulda backed ye if'n ye wanted te take him on. Ye know that, don't ye? We coulda whipped his ass good!"

Sam Cohen grins and nods his head.

"Yeah, I know we could've whipped him good, Joe. That ain't the point. Logan has a lot of friends in this territory, and he's friends with the law as well. You see all these men in the saloon? We don't stand a chance against all o' them, and they would've come to his rescue, make no mistake about that. Naw, our paths'll cross again sooner or later. He has his day comin.'"

The four men laugh softly.

"That's why we like ridin' with you, Sam; there's always some action to look forward to."

Sam cautions his ranch hands to keep calm.

"Alright, alright; simmer down! We don't want the entire town to know about our plans, so watch what you say from now on. Let's go have us a beer. This round's on me. After that each one o' you is gonna buy me a drink."

The four cowhands look at one another in alarm and start protesting wildly.

"That ain't fair, Sam! Ye can't just ..."

"Well, either you pay up now, or I'll just take it off your weeks' wages; problem solved! How's that sound?"

"No, no! Sam, ye don't touch our wages; each of us'll buy you a drink, okay?"

Sam is elated.

"Now that's more like it! An' that's why I enjoy hangin' out with you guys; you're always so generous!"

There are smirks and a few unfavorable words are mumbled which makes Sam smile as he catches a word here and there. Nothing he can't fix with a little hard labor.

Charlie is waiting as the group of men closed in on the bar counter. He places their beers in front of them and holds out his hand.

"Pay up now, Sam. I ain't givin' you a tab till the end of the evenin' again like the last time. As a matter of fact; you still owe me twenty-five dollars. Altogether it'll be thirty dollars you gotta pay me now. If you don't have the money, get up an' get out!"

"Whoa, Charlie! Darn it, keep your pants on; I'll pay up what I owe you. Gettin' excited like that over a few dollars'll get you nowhere but six feet under. All you had to do was ask me politely. How long do we know each other? Feels like a million years!"

Sam hands over the thirty dollars and turns laughingly to the ranch hands, raising his glass.

"Cheers men! Let's drink to us; there ain't nothin' else worth drinkin' to."

The Double Diamond Ranch. Lucinda Walker stands on the wide veranda of her parents' house, taking in all the splendor of the early-morning sunrise as dawn breaks over the landscape. There's a light, refreshing breeze that rustles the leaves.

Lucy, as her friends and parents call her, is beautiful. Her skin is velvet soft and smooth, and a healthy tan gives it the glow of golden honey. Lucy's hair is long and golden-blond, with blue-green eyes and long lashes. Her lips are soft and full, and her smile reveals perfect milk-white teeth.

Both Logan and Lucy are in the same class since grade school, and it stays that way throughout their entire school careers. They become aware of each other romantically when they reach their teens. Logan doesn't wait, and soon they are a couple.

Lucy becomes an extremely beautiful girl when she reaches her teenage years and later on as a young woman. She's been blessed with a slender figure.

Lost in her thoughts, Lucy is caught unawares when her father suddenly speaks up behind her.

"I'll give you a dime for each one of your thoughts, honey."

"Daddy! You almost gave me a heart attack. You're going to have to come up with a lot of dimes!"

Both laugh at this remark. Dan Walker looks at his daughter in admiration. He adores her to bits, and likes to spoil her. He is ever thankful that Lucy is back with them for good this time. There was a time when both Dan and his wife had lost all hope that they'd ever see Lucy alive again.

"When last did you see Logan, honey? He's been awfully scarce these last couple of weeks."

Lucy nods her head in answer to her father's question.

"Yes, he's been rather absent, hasn't he, daddy? I think I'll take a ride out to his place a little later on to see how he's doing. Do you want to go along for the ride?"

Dan shakes his head in denial.

"Sorry, honey; I'll have to take a raincheck on that. Gotta help your mama with some chores. She wants to go into town and get some supplies, so I'm taking her with the buckboard."

Lucy hugs Dan and smiles at him.

"Don't worry, daddy; that's fine. I'm a big girl, and I always enjoy taking a ride by myself. Anyway, it's not that far."

Dan excuses himself and crosses over to the bunkhouse where the ranch hands sleep. Lucy thinks back to when she decided to go to Logan's ranch he bought only two weeks previously.

It's the first time she visits there, as Logan first wants to purchase a few head of cattle and some horses. He is also adamant to get a house built before he shows her the ranch. When she asks him why, he answers in his calm way with laughter twinkling in his eyes.

"Oh, just to make it a little more homely, you know? I couldn't let you come and visit me on an empty piece of land!"

Lucy jokes around with Logan, playing along. She puts her face next to his and whispers in his ear with her soft Tinkerbell voice.

"Really? Do you think it's going to make a difference if you put some livestock on your land?"

Logan gets goosebumps from head to toes. She is irresistible and knows exactly how to get him revved up. He encircles her waist, pulling her in closer.

"Yeah, miss Walker. I'm buildin' us a house right over there, with a veranda and kitchen as big as you want. The stables will be over there, and a huge corral right next to it where your horses can roam around freely. I'll get you as many horses as you like. What do you think about that?"

Lucy likes the sound of that.

"It sounds breathtakingly beautiful; exactly the way I like it. You make me so happy! Have I told you how much I love you?"

"You have, but you can tell me again."

Logan kisses Lucy passionately. She stares up into his eyes.

"What are you going to name your ranch; thought of a name yet?"

"As a matter of fact, I have. Think I'll call it the Circle Double-L; both our names combined. Do you like it?"

Lucy wrinkles her nose at Logan and laughs for joy.

"I like it; it sounds so successful!"

They lose track of time after that ...

CHAPTER TWO

Five years previously; dusk, somewhere in West Texas.

The horse that enters the larger-than-average town has lost its spunk; almost dragging its body on hooves that are short of three ironclad shoes. A figure resembling that of a young female, struggles to keep herself in the saddle while holding onto the pommel to do so.

What catches the eyes are the twin low-slung six-shooters riding her hips on either side. A second glance at the girl will leave a man astonished at her beauty, something not noticeable at first glance. Her clothes are trail-worn and dirty; dust and sweat mingling to form a thin-layered crust on her skin.

Reaching the Livery, the girl sits astride her mount for a moment before dismounting. The Liveryman stands idly by and waits. He sees that the figure has difficulty in standing alone and tries to lend a helping hand. Cautiously taking hold of the rider's arm, he speaks in a gentle manner.

"You alright, mister? Pardon me for sayin' so, but you look like shit. You want me te take care o' your hoss for you? I'd be glad to help ye get te the Hotel. We can talk about payin' me for your hoss tomorrow; when you feel better."

The figure reacts suddenly and without warning, exploding into a ball of fiery fury and shakes off the hand that holds its arm.

"I'm no mister, you idiot! If you call me that again, I'll pump you so full of lead your coffin'll be too heavy to carry! Just take care of my mount; I'm alright. I'll square up with you tomorrow for a stable and food for my horse."

The voice catches the Liveryman by surprise. He looks again and realizes the entity of his mistake. He is caught by the blaze of fire in the bluest eyes he's ever come across, followed by a dirty, but nonetheless, beautiful face. A Stetson is pulled down low to conceal most of the features. Those guns are ...

"Oh, my gosh! I'm sorry, miss; did'n realize you was a lady."

"That's fine, mister. Don't sweat it. Just show me in the direction of a Hotel where I can find good food and a hot bath."

Without further hesitation, the Liveryman points in the direction of the closest Hotel. She takes her saddlebags, rifle and bedroll and stumbles in the direction of the Hotel. The clerk avoids any eye contact and pushes the key of her room carefully towards her over the counter.

The Hotel clerk hates violence of any sort and one look at the figure standing in front of him, convinces him that she's trouble with a capital T. On top of it all; she's a woman, and woman who carry guns like those riding their hips so low ... The clerk glances sidelong at the new tenants clothing and wrinkles his nose.

A woolen shirt and denim; boots scuffed beyond recognition of their color. The trench coat catches the clerk's attention. Although it's dirty and caked with dirt and sweat, it's obviously very expensive, and speaks of good taste.

The woman takes her key and ascends the stairs to the first landing. Halfway up the stairs she turns and requests information from him.

"Could you have some food sent to my room? I'd appreciate it, thank you."

Without waiting for an answer, she turns and disappears from sight.

Known amongst others of the same trade as herself, other outlaws and gunfighters fear Remi Dodge as one of the fastest guns. She's killed at least a dozen men and is a wanted Outlaw in several states. That's why she has fled to this remote part of Texas. She's unknown around these parts. Maybe she can wait it out and lay low until the dust has settled.

Remi lies in bed listening to the noises outside in the street. It's seven o' clock and for once she enjoys the luxury of sleeping late. The sun shines brightly through her window. As she lies there, Remi's thoughts return to the life she left behind because nothing mattered anymore.

She thinks about her parents a lot nowadays. She misses them, but also knows that she can't return home, as her father doesn't condone her way of life. Then there's the love of her life; Logan. He chose to go to war when he had the choice of choosing between her and the Army. Her heart aches when she thinks of him, and how happy they were.

She's chosen another name for herself, one that will not bring her family name in jeopardy. The thought of ending this nomadic lifestyle often enters her mind. She's tired of the constant running from the Law and looking over her shoulder for the next gunslinger who thinks that he can outdraw her.

Remi gets out of bed and dresses in a clean pair of denim, which has also seen better days. At least she can take the clothing she wore while travelling here and get them cleaned.

Rolling the clothing into a bundle, Remi descends the stairs into the Hotel lobby. Remi isn't wearing her Stetson and her long brushed hair reaches to her waist. Her appearance brings about plenty of admiring stares from men passing through the lobby. This is also something Remi has become accustomed to. Remi opts to disregard it.

Remi leaves the Hotel and walks over to the dry-cleaning store, where she hands her clothing in for proper cleaning. She heads back to the Hotel for breakfast, as she is famished after having a good night's rest. After breakfast, Remi goes to the Livery where she finds the same man from the previous evening.

"Good mornin', ma'am. Hope you had a good night's rest. Your hoss has been washed and fed. I put her back yonder where there's less noise. She's a real beaut."

Remi smiles; a rare occurrence of lately. She loves horses, and complimenting her horse, means you're a good person by heart according to her standards.

"Yes, she is special. Thank you for taking such good care of her. Please get the Blacksmith to put some shoes on her hooves. This should cover it."

Remi hands the handler a fistful of dollars.

"Take what I owe you out of that money and pay the Blacksmith. If there's any change, keep it."

The handler is in awe with the amount of money he's received.

"Thank you, ma'am. How long you plan on stayin' around town? It ain't none o' my business, but if ye plan on stayin' fer long, I'll put her in a large cubicle where she has enough space to move around a little."

Remi nods her head.

"Yes, that sounds good; do it."

Without any further conversation, Remi leaves the livery. She enters the hardware store to purchase an extra denim and shirts as well as a new pair of boots. While deciding what boots to choose, Remi looks up and notices a man staring at her. He walks towards her, stopping a few feet from Remi.

"My, my; isn't this a coincidence! Didn't think we'd ever meet way out here, Remi. What you doing so far West by the way; hiding out?"

Remi's eyes are cold as she stares back at the man. He's an old rival of hers; one she wishes she can make disappear, but alas. Remi can't shake him; he always seems to sniff her out.

"I could ask you the same question, Kid. Don't owe you an explanation for anything I do or where I go. Stay out of my way! You won't be so lucky next time."

Kid Colt feigns the shocked expression on his face.

"Remi, we're friends! I'd never do anything to stir up trouble with you. It's pure luck us being in the same town at the same time. I got your back, and I'd feel a lot safer if I knew you had mine. Can we at least agree on that?"

"The only thing I'll agree to is to let you live; as long as you stay out of my sight. If you as much as try to chat me up again, consider yourself challenged!"

Remi turns her back on the man she knows as Kid and strides out into the warm mid-morning sun. His gaze follows her all the way to the Hotel entrance. Then he shrugs the conversation off as a bad experience. Kid nonetheless heeds the warning he's received from Remi. He doesn't know her to make idle threats.

XXX

Sheriff Jesse Truman stands in his office at the window, looking out over the town. The mug of strong black coffee he holds in his hand tastes foul. He has just warmed up yesterday's brew.

"Tastes like shit! This stuff'll kill me before I grow old", he mutters under his breath. His keen eyesight catches and recognizes Kid just as he ascends the steps and enters the hardware store. There is a wanted poster out for him with a large reward on his head; dead or alive.

Jesse is of average build and length, light-brown hair and a suntanned complexion with green eyes and ruggedly handsome features. He is very handy with a gun, but not stupid enough to take on a gunslinger like Kid. He'll have to call in the help of his Deputies to try to disarm Colt before incarcerating him. Sheriff Truman knows however, that he will have to make his presence known to the gunman.

Sheriff Jesse Truman seats himself in a chair on the boardwalk outside the hardware store. He's a patient man. He rolls a cigarette and strikes a match to it. The cigarette is almost finished, when the door to the store is flung open with tremendous force.

It happens so fast that Jesse almost swallows his cigarette with fright. He regains his composure and sees a young woman exit the store in a hurry, obviously dissatisfied with something. Jesse tries contemplating the cause behind the young woman's behavior, when the door opens again and Kid appears. He walks a few steps before Jesse's voice stops him.

"That's far enough, Colt! I could arrest you right now, but I ain't stupid enough to try. Although I'm fast, I know you'll outdraw me first chance you get, and I ain't ready to meet my maker yet. Tell me what you're doin' in my town, and make the story stick!"

Kid slowly makes half a turn. The first thing he notices is the five-point star pinned to the shirt front of the man facing him. Kid is allergic to Lawmen. He's always been in trouble with the Law; ever since he can remember. Even as a young boy the law seemed to be against his very existence.

"Sheriff, very glad to meet you! I was going to come and introduce myself, but I see it isn't necessary. How do you know my name, and what do you have against me being in your town?"

Jesse Truman raises himself from the chair and goes to stand opposite Kid, looking him squarely in the eye.

"I'm not playing that game with you, Colt. Like I said; there's a wanted poster of you in my office. The bounty on your head's a large one, and that could attract the wrong kind of people here. I don't have any trouble with any of my citizens in the county and I don't intend to start now. Once people around here find out who you are, they'll turn into an angry mob. Your life won't be worth shit, so I suggest you keep your stay as short as possible; for both our sakes."

Kid hooks his thumbs into his gun belt and a laconic smile plays around the corners of his mouth.

"Sheriff, believe me when I say I'm not thrilled to meet you. The truth of the matter is I actually just stopped off here to get some supplies. I've changed my mind in the meantime; think I'll stay a day or two."

Jesse and the gunman stare unblinkingly at one another. Jesse breaks the silence.

"I don't want to see you in my town after two days, mister Colt. If I do, you'll become a household name and hunted down. Two days, Colt. Don't cause trouble in my town with those."

Jesse points to the side arms holstered to Kid's hips. Kid makes a gun with his thumb and forefinger.

"Got it, Lawman! I might even be on my way by tomorrow. Have yourself a good day!"

Kid Colt turns around and walks off towards the saloon. Jesse watches him, his mind working overtime. He will have to be watched closely.

REMI IS BESIDE HERSELF with anger. She came here in the hope that she would find peace; at least for a while. Now she's stuck with one of her biggest rivals. Remi hopes that he will heed her warning and steer clear of her.

She feels like a drink, and decides to have only one. The Hotel's restaurant is still closed, which means she'll have to go to the saloon. Remi doesn't like saloons. Men are of a mind that women who drink in a saloon, are out looking only for one thing. Remi detests that.

Remi quickly makes her way to the saloon closest to the Hotel. Entering it, she stands just inside the batwing doors looking for a suitable place to sit down. She notices an empty chair at the far end of the bar counter and heads for it. At first everything seems to go well, until a young man, intoxicated, notices her and whistles.

"Hey, missy; come on over here so's I can show you what a real man can do for you! Promise it won't hurt none if you play along. Wait till I get my hands on you; you'll be beggin' me for more!"

It's too late to turn around. Remi knows that she'll have to stick it out until she has finished her drink. Calm and collectively she takes her place at the bar counter, smiling at the barman. He smiles back and whispers to Remi.

"Don't pay him any attention, missy; he's drunk as a skunk, and a jerk. What can I bring you?"

"I'll have a good Whisky, please; a single with milk."

The barman nods his head, pouring her drink in front of her. He places a jug filled with milk in front of Remi.

"There you go, missy. You can pour the milk, if you don't mind. I don't want to add too much or too little. You know how you prefer it."

"Thanks, barkeep; how much do I owe you?"

Remi pulls money from her pocket, but the barman waves it away.

"This one's on the house, miss; don't worry about it."

Remi smiles and lifts her glass.

"Thank you once again. I need this one."

Remi throws her head back and empties her glass with no effort. She turns and walks towards the exit. A familiar face suddenly blocks her path. Remi tries to push past him, but he won't budge. She shoves him, and he staggers back.

"I told you to stay the hell away from me, Kid! Seems like you're out looking for trouble, aren't you? Well, I'm happy to oblige. Call it!"

The saloon goes gravely silent, every eye on the neatly dressed man facing Remi. Kid smiles and steps back while he retorts loudly.

"Not now, Remi. I've had a mite too many drinks. I'll challenge you tomorrow at noon on town square. Have a good night's rest; you're gonna need it!"

Remi puts her face right up against that of Kid, speaking in a clear voice.

"I accept. Don't keep me waiting tomorrow!"

Remi pushes past Kid, spilling some of his drink on the floor. There is a buzz of excited voices as she leaves the saloon, and Remi knows that word will spread faster than a wildfire.

19

CHAPTER THREE

Jesse Truman's sleep evades him during the night. He rolls around and is restless throughout, as he has a gut feeling that Kid is here to make trouble. His wife makes him several cups of hot Cocoa; to no avail. Jesse is up and dressed at four o' clock in the morning, and tells his wife that he's going to the office.

A ways off Jesse notices that the office light is off, and knows what it means. Reaching the office, Jesse opens the door and puts the light switch on. His deputy lies back in the chair with his feet stretched out in front of him on the desk.

Jesse is furious. Anything can happen and his Deputy won't even know about it! Jesse slams down hard on the desk with an open palm.

"Rodney, wake up!"

The bang is so loud and sudden that it jolts Rodney from his deep sleep. He kicks his feet straight, causing the chair to tilt backwards. Rodney lands on the hardwood floor, yelling as he gets up in a daze.

"What the hell ..., who fired that shot? I'm comin', I'm comin'! Take cover!"

When Rodney realizes that it's Jesse, he becomes speechless and just takes a seat, his head in his hands. He is rather pale. Jesse can't help but laugh at the expression on Rodney's face. It lightens Jesse's mood somewhat.

"Well, I guess that'll teach you not to sleep again while you're doing the graveyard shift, huh? What if a robber came in here and shot you all to hell? I know it's difficult to keep awake during night time, but when I appoint the new Deputy, you also get to sleep at home nights. No more nightshift, alright? Just hold out for a couple more nights."

Rodney's color returns to his face. He shakes his head and makes a meek attempt at laughing. It doesn't work.

"Yeah, thanks Jesse. Sorry man; I was tired, you know. Never happened before. Why you here so early?"

Jesse waves it away.

"That's alright, Rodney. Forget about it. I couldn't sleep either. I told you I ran into Kid Colt yesterday, right? Well, the thing is; I know there's trouble brooding, coz he is trouble. I just don't know what or who. You can go home now. I ain't gonna sleep again, so you might's well use the opportunity while I'm offering it to you."

xxx

Morning comes quick and hot. Jesse can't remember when last he's seen the town wake up and come alive. The fresh morning air is revitalizing. Most citizens are surprised to see Jesse up and about so early. They hardly ever see him before ten or eleven o'clock in the morning. Paperwork keeps Jesse busy for the most part of the day.

Jesse starts his rounds just after eight thirty. He walks slowly through town to stop every now and then to chat with citizens. Jesse doesn't know whether it's his imagination or not, but he senses a feeling of anxious anticipation from especially some of the townsmen he speaks to.

Asking around casually, Jesse determines that it will be better to ask Burt, the barman. Jesse waits for the saloon to open, and at exactly ten o' clock the doors open for business. Burt sings like a canary, disclosing every last detail to Jesse. He also makes it clear that it seems the lady knows the man who has challenged her.

With thirty minutes to spare before the gunfight, Jesse rushes to the town square, where he finds almost half of the town's citizens waiting.

Ten minutes to twelve Kid shows up. He is full of himself, boasting that he is unbeatable. Shooting off at the mouth, he adds that the woman he is about to shoot, is also a famous gunslinger, and feared by plenty of the same profession.

This is news to Jesse. Hearing her name from Kid doesn't jog Jesse's memory of ever having seen a wanted poster of her. The crowd has grown immensely and they are hanging on Kid's every word. The bell tower strikes twelve, and Kid's face glows with self-righteousness as he gloats.

"You see; what did I tell you just a few minutes ago? She's too scared to face me, 'cause she knows I'm too fast for her! Now everyone'll know what a yellow belly she really is! I'll spread the word where ever I go. She'll be the laughing stock!"

The crowd falls silent all at once. From their midst steps Remi, quietly taking in all the accusations slandered by Kid Colt. Kid becomes aware that someone else is in the arena with him. Turning around, he stares in shocked recognition at the figure standing twenty paces from him. He tries to make amends.

"Remi, I, I didn't ..."

"You said it, Kid. I'm here; let's do this. You will never have the opportunity again, so use it while you can."

Remi mesmerizes Jesse as he looks at her. She is dressed in her gunslinger's attire. From the tip of her Stetson to the toe of her new boots, she looks breathtaking. Her long blond hair blows lightly in the soft breeze. Jesse knows that he can't, no; doesn't want to stop this gunfight.

Kid knows there is no turning back now. He laughs sarcastically and moves his legs a little apart.

"You sure you're up to this, Remi? This is your chance to still get out in one piece. No? Such a pity; I didn't really want to do this ..."

Kid Colt's hand streaks down like a lightning bolt. His gun clears leather in one smooth motion, hammer pulled back. Jesse watches

Remi when he sees Kid going for his gun. Neither Jesse nor anyone else sees Remi draw. She fires both her guns simultaneously before Kid can squeeze off one shot.

Both bullets hit Kid in the chest, lifting him off his feet and flinging him backwards. He dies when the bullets enter his body; dead before he is flung back by the impact. Remi holsters her guns, turns around and walks away.

Jesse knows he has to talk to her before she disappears, and sets out after her. Passing the undertaker's, Jesse goes in and orders the undertaker to fetch the body at town square. Exiting the funeral parlor, he is just in time to see Remi enter the Hotel.

Jesse barges into the Hotel's foyer and rings the bell on the counter. The clerk, a young boy, emerges from the office holding a newspaper in his hand. When he sees Jesse, his smile fades.

"Can I ..."

"What's the room number of that young lady? She just came in here a few minutes ago!"

"Uhm, I ..."

"Never mind, Albert!" Jesse exclaims as he goes up the stairs two at a time. A door at the end of the hallway closes just as Jesse reaches the first landing. Getting his breath back, Jesse slowly closes the distance to where he sees the door close. He knocks three times and listens.

Jesse hears footsteps and stands back from the door. When the door opens, Jesse and Remi stare at each other for a couple of seconds. Before Jesse can move, he is covered by two six-guns. He raises his hands, getting goosebumps all over his body.

"Whoa now, lady; take it easy! I didn't come here to make trouble for you. I'm Sheriff Jesse Truman. I heard what Kid said about you, but I ain't interested in taking you down. You actually did me a favor. I'm here to tell you that Kid had a large bounty on his head; dead or alive. He was free game, so you can claim the bounty. It's a lot of money;

twenty thousand dollars! Come by the office tomorrow; I'll have the cash ready for you."

Remi is watching Jesse like a hawk. Slowly she lets her gun hand down before she holsters the gun. The door to her Hotel room is still open and she beckons for Jesse to enter.

"Come inside, Sheriff. Sorry about that, but I'm not exactly on the right side of the Law. I'm packing my things and moving out. Actually, to tell you the truth; this gunfight couldn't have happened at a more convenient time in my life. I wasn't looking for anything like this to happen, but it helped me make up my mind about my life. I'm tired of running and living in constant fear of being recognized by some wannabe gunslinger who wants to shoot it out with me. I've killed enough men to last me a lifetime. My conscience is getting the better of me, and I miss my parents. I'm going home. My parents are old and don't deserve a daughter who's an Outlaw. What I'm saying is that I'm hanging up my guns for good. My boyfriend and the other citizens of my hometown don't know about this part of my life, and I'd like to keep it that way."

"That sure is some story, miss. For my own curiosity; who are you? Your name didn't ring a bell, and I don't have a wanted poster of you, so's far as I'm concerned, you're just a regular Jane who shot a gunslinger in self-defense."

"Thank you, Sheriff. My name is Remi Dodge, just like Kid said. We were big archenemies, the two of us. You'd think because we were in the same line of work we'd be friends or something similar. I once witnessed him kill a woman and her child without batting an eye or having a second's remorse. I've hated his guts ever since that day. I've never killed for the sheer fun of it, nor for the rush it brings. I can't give you a legitimate reason why I started this line of work in the first place."

Jesse watches her while she speaks, and he can see as well as hear the remorse in her voice. He nods his head in agreement.

"Yeah, I can understand you and Kid being enemies in the same circle. I've heard a lot of bad things about him. I don't blame you for killing him today. You were a big help to society. You can be at my office bright-and-early tomorrow morning for the reward. Enjoy the rest of your day."

Jesse turns and leaves the room. Remi stares after him in disbelief. She had seen him follow her from the gunfight, and had prepared to finish him off as well, had it been necessary. She is glad that things turned out the way it did.

Finishing her packing, she leaves the Hotel and walks over to the telegraph office. Here she quickly writes a telegram and asks the clerk to send it to the office in her hometown. Having a reason to live again, she leaves the telegraph office smiling. Nobody need ever know her secret ...

CHAPTER FOUR

Reaching Logan's ranch, and her thoughts back on track, Lucy looks around expecting to see Logan busy building their home alongside his crew. Surprised not to find him there, Lucy walks over to where his foreman is busy marking off some measurements.

"Hey, Mike; is Logan around? I don't see him anywhere."

Mike Fuller stops what he is doing and turns to face Lucy. He is awestruck every time he sees her.

"Hi, miss Walker. I'm fine; thank you for asking. Yeah; sorry to disappoint you, but Logan's stayin' over in town for a week. He sent a stable hand from the Livery over with a message this afternoon. He's over at the hotel. Said he'll be back again sometime next week after he's sorted out a problem. Asked me to give you this."

Mike holds out an envelope addressed to Lucy. Lucy lets her eyes fly over the one short page of words.

"Sweetheart

I apologize from my heart for having to cancel our date tonight, since I know how much it means to both of us. There's something I have to take care of in town, so I'll be staying at the Hotel for a couple of days. Tell you all about it when I'm back home. See you soon. Love, Logan."

"Thank you, Mike. Enjoy the rest of the week."

"It's a pleasure, Miss Walker. See you when Logan gets back."

Mounting her Arabian Appaloosa, Lucy lets her gaze wonder over the land one last time before swinging her Mare in the direction of their own ranch.

Lucy knows Logan as well as he does himself, and knows with certainty that he won't cancel their date without having a plausible reason. A thought strikes her.

"Now why can't I stop by the Hotel and visit Logan there?"

This makes sense to Lucy the more she thinks about it. Yep, that's what she will do. She'll surprise Logan. Lucy is sure he'll appreciate the gesture.

XXX

Lucy reaches the ranch about an hour before her parents arrive home. She is packing a small suitcase when her mother enters her room. Brenda Walker is every bit as beautiful as Lucy although she is in her deep forties. Her figure is also still in good shape. Brenda looks amazed when she notices the suitcase.

"Going somewhere, baby?"

"Oh, hello mama. I didn't hear you come in. Yes, I went to Logan's' this morning, but he wasn't there. He has some business in town that needs some taking care of, so I thought I'd surprise him by paying him a visit at the Hotel. D'you think he'd like that?"

Brenda throws her head back and laughs.

"Oh, Lucy! You're terrible, and that's why we all love you so much, including Logan. Of course he'll be surprised! He would have been coming here tonight to visit you if I'm not mistaken?"

Lucy smiles as she looks up at her mother.

"Yes, mama, Logan was supposed to come here tonight. He apologized for not being able to make it, so that's why I'm going into town. Do you and daddy mind?"

Brenda's eyes are soft as she looks at her only daughter and shakes her head.

"No, of course not, my darling. Enjoy the weekend. When can we expect you to be back?"

"I'll be home Sunday afternoon, mama. Say around four o' clock."

Brenda Walker nods her head in agreement.

"That's fine, my darling. I'll make something special for you when you return."

It's Lucy's turn to laugh.

"Mama, you're going to make me put on weight the way you carry on! I'll become a spinster, and you'll be stuck with me."

With both women now laughing, they walk down the passage towards the kitchen. Here they find Dan seated at the table with a mug of strong, steaming coffee in his hand. He looks up when the two women enter. Dan points at the stove.

"Just in time! Can I pour you ladies each a cup of my delicious brew?"

"Thank you, daddy. That will be nice. Your coffee's strong enough to conquer the worst thirst."

Dan pours Lucy a cup of coffee and hands it to her. He notices the small suitcase on the table.

"What's this, honey; you going somewhere?"

"Yes, daddy; I thought I'd surprise Logan. He's in town for a while, and I have nothing to do at home. Mama said it's alright if I go. I'll be home Sunday afternoon around four, alright? Oh, I wanted to ask you; would it be alright if I took the buckboard? It'll be a little uncomfortable with my baggage on a horse."

Dan pushes his chair back and gets up He walks to where Lucy is standing and hugs her.

"You don't need to ask permission to use the buggy, honey, and as long as we know where you are, you're free to come and go as you wish. Give Logan our regards and enjoy the weekend."

"Thanks, daddy."

Dan and Brenda accompany Lucy to where the buckboard is standing. Dan puts Lucy's suitcase aboard the buckboard and hugs her again. Brenda also takes her turn.

Lucy disentangles herself from Brenda's embrace, laughing as she does so.

"Mama, I'm back on Sunday, and town's half an hour's ride. Enjoy your weekend."

With a light pluck of the reigns, the buckboard begins rolling. Lucy lifts her arm and waves.

"Bye, mama, daddy. See you on Sunday!

XXX

The high clock tower reads 12:15PM when Lucy rides into town and dismounts in front of the Hotel. She takes her suitcase from the seat of the buckboard and ascends the four steps onto the Hotel boardwalk.

Lucy enters the foyer and walks up to the information desk, where she rings the bell on the tabletop for service. A young girl appears, greeting her with a friendly smile.

"Hi, miss Walker. It's good to see you a-gain. You haven't been in town for a while."

Lucy returns the favor with a wide smile.

"Hello, Belle. Yes, I've been a little busy. How are you doing?"

"I'm fine, thank you. How can I help you today?"

Lucy smiles mischievously.

"Well, Logan's staying at the Hotel, but you ought to know that. He doesn't know I'm here, so I'd like to surprise him. What's his room number?"

Belle hesitates. Although everybody knows Lucy well in these parts, the Hotel has a strict policy regarding information about Hotel guests.

"Uhm, well, I don't think he's in his room, Miss Walker. Let me ..."

"Oh, that's alright, Belle. I'll just go on up and wait for him; if you can please give me a spare key for his room. Don't tell him that I'm waiting for him, alright? That'll spoil the surprise."

Lucy holds out her hand for the spare key to the room. Belle looks around, anticipating the manager to turn up at any moment. She shakes her head.

"I really am very sorry, miss Walker, but you know what the Hotel's policy is. The Manager is very strict about things like that and if I'm caught disobeying the rules, I'll lose my job."

Lucy sighs and opens her handbag. She takes out several dollar bills and pushes it over the counter to the clerk.

"Take this, Belle. There's fifty dollars there; more than you make in two months. Now; can I please have the key to Logan's room? I promise I won't tell a soul if you don't."

Belle hesitates briefly before she turns around and takes a key from the board behind her.

Alright, but if you get caught, I'll deny everything."

Lucy takes the key from Belle and smiles. Belle watches Lucy as she ascends the stairs to the second floor. Lucy finds the room number easily, and without further ado, unlocks the door and enters.

Lucy places her suitcase on the chair and sitting down on the bed, removes her boots. She rubs her feet and pulls a face.

Lying down on the large bed, Lucy closes her eyes for a brief second ...

In her dream, Logan is smothering her with kisses, repeating her name over-and-over again.

"Wake up, honey; Lucy!"

Lucy slowly opens her eyes to find that Logan is leaning over her, and planting kisses on her face and lips. Confused, she sits up.

"What, what happened? You weren't here a couple of seconds ago when I arrived!"

Logan laughs, stroking her hair.

"No honey, I wasn't here when you arrived. Imagine my surprise when I opened my door and found you asleep on my bed! That was two hours ago. You must've been tired, coz you arrived about an hour before I returned. You slept like a baby for about three hours, and I couldn't get it over my heart to wake you."

Lucy blushes.

"I'm sorry, Logan. I wanted to surprise you, and then you surprise me!"

Logan shakes his head.

"Oh no, believe me when I say you surprised me really good! You were the last person I expected here, but I'm not complaining. I'm glad you came. You staying until Sunday, I hope?"

Lucy is fully awake by now, a look of surprise on her beautiful features.

"Of course I'm staying until Sunday, that's to say if you want me to. Oh, my goodness, the buckboard's still standing out front!"

Lucy jumps up off the bed. Logan calms her down.

"Now don't go worryin' your pretty head over none of that, honey. I took care of it. The horse has been stabled and fed, and the buck-board's parked away safely."

"Thank you, baby. That's why I appreciate you so much."

"Don't mention it. I'm glad you came. Sorry about me not pitching at your father's ranch tonight."

"I was going to ask you what the reason was behind your stay in town. You didn't say anything about staying over in town the last time we spoke. I went out to your ranch this morning and was there when the stable hand arrived with your message for Mike. That's when I decided to ride into town and surprise you."

"I was in the saloon when old Frank was hauled in, beat up bad by Sam and three of his ranch hands. Well, then I took him to the Doc's house to be examined. Doc says old Frank took a very brutal beating and as a result suffered some nasty damage. They broke his right forearm, most o' the bones in his face, includin' his jaw and nose, as well as a couple of his ribs. He has to stay in bed for at least a week while Doc treats him."

"I don't understand, baby; what's all this have to do with you? It's bad about old Franks' beating and all, but what can you do about it?"

"Well honey, I thought I could take Frank to the ranch and give him a chance to make something of himself. I'll get Mike and the other cowhands to show him the ropes. He'll be gettin' a weekly wage, free food an' a bed to sleep in. I reckon he'll fit right in."

Lucy wraps her arms around Logan's neck and hugs him tight.

"Well, if I was old Frank and someone offered me an opportunity like that, I'd surely take it. You're most probably paying for his treatment too, the way I know you."

"The Doc also has to make a livin'. Besides, it's goin' to take old Frank a long time to get back to his old self, an' what better place to revive his spirit than the Double L?"

Lucy nods her head.

"You're right, baby. That'll give him the chance to sober up too. I hope Frank realizes how much he has to be thankful for with you on his side."

"Frank's not a bad person, honey. There just hasn't been anybody willin' to help him. Enough said about Frank. What would you like to do tonight?"

Lucy thinks about this for a moment.

"I think we should have a quiet evening indoors. Let's get room service. After dinner I'm going to have a nice hot bath, then you can start spoiling me."

Logan smiles from ear to ear.

"Yeah, sounds good! I couldn't have said it better. Let's go have us something to drink in the meantime."

Chapter FIVE

Late Friday afternoon; Sam Cohen's ranch.

Sam is looking through his binoculars when he notices the buckboard kick up dust on the trail miles from his ranch. The binoculars in his hands are very powerful; left to him by his late granddad. He isn't interested in the buckboard, but rather in the occupant.

Sam feels the lust in him well up as he watches the figure in the driver's seat. He's always had a thing for Lucy Walker; since childhood. She has never paid him any attention, though. Through the years he's tried desperately to win her over, but there has always been one boy, and later, man, to keep reckoning with; Logan Prescott.

Sam is aware of more than one way that he loathes Logan! There is Logan's' characteristics. It attracts people young and old, and all the young women in the area are after Logan's company. It's more than he, Sam, can say. Sam thinks back to when they were very young children.

Him and Logan, as well as Lucy, were very good friends, played together, were mischievous together. Sam lived with his parents on this same ranch, his father a cattle-breeder.

Then something goes terribly wrong one day for no known reason. His father comes home from town as drunk as a skunk. Taking out his six-gun, he shoots his wife at point blank range, then turns the gun on himself.

A ranch hand hears the gunshots and comes across the nasty scene. A letter is mailed to Sam's granddad, who arrives two days later. He finds Sam sitting in his parents' room, silently observing a photo of his mother.

Sam's life changes for the worst after the fateful incident. In school, the children push him aside, treating him like a Leper. Under the impression that Logan is amongst those who cast him aside, Sam keeps his once best friend at a distance. This causes alienation between them, and Lucinda choses to stay at Logan's side.

Their friendship shattered, Sam grows up a recluse. His demeanor is bitter and hateful, and he is in trouble more times than he can remember. His granddad tries to put a leash on his behavior, to no avail. He is too old, and can't handle the rough-spirited youngster. Sam turns out to be a troublemaker and is very unpopular with the other students. He's been dealt a bad hand.

Sam is yanked back to the here and now. Watching the buckboard as it disappears over a hill, Sam wonders why Lucy is heading for town. He shrugs his shoulders. It's none of his concern.

But when Sam thinks about it, he realizes that Lucy is going to be all by herself. If he accidentally meets her in town, it will give him the opportunity to speak to her alone.

Shouting to one of the cowhands to saddle his horse, Sam dresses in his neatest attire and takes to the trail, following Lucy at a distance.

Sam can't wait to meet up with Lucy and spend an evening in her company ...

XXX

Logan and Lucy go downstairs to the Hotel restaurant, where Logan orders them each a cold beverage. A tall man enters the restaurant and looks around the room.

Logan lifts his arm and waves.

"How are you doing, Lew? Looking for someone in particular?"

Sheriff Lew Parker waves back and comes towards their table, a wide smile on his friendly face.

"Now ain't this somethin' sweet for the eye. I don't mean you, Logan!"

The two men laugh and shake hands. Sheriff Parker tips his Stetson at Lucy.

"Always good to see you, Lucy. Haven't seen you two lovebirds in quite some time. How's the ranchin' comin' along, Logan; the house standin' yet?"

Logan shakes his head.

"Naw, I ain't that lucky. Building a ranch is hard work, but I'm getting there. By the time Lucy and I get hitched, everything'll be in place. Who you lookin' for?"

Lew Parker's facial expression changes from friendly to disgruntled.

"Heck, I been lookin' for Sam now for the past three days, but it seems he's left town an' gone back to his ranch. 'Bout an hour ago someone told me he's in town. Went to the saloon to have a look, but he ain't there. Doc Ford informed me on Wednesday mornin' about the attack on old Frank. Sam better have an explanation ready for me, an' if it ain't a good one, he'll be spendin' the weekend in my cells!"

"Yeah, old Frank took quite a beating, alright. I'm surprised he doesn't have more injuries!"

"You know about the attack on Frank?"

Logan nods his head affirmatively.

"Sure do. I was in the saloon when Sam an' three of his ranch hands haul old Frank into the saloon. Sam wasn't too pleased when I inter-vened."

Sheriff Parker's face is one of astonishment.

"Do you know why he beat the hell out of ole Frank, coz nobody else seems to know anything. Seems he's up to somethin', and I'd like to know what it is."

Logan replies affirmatively.

"Yeah, Sam seemed a little edgy Lew; know what I mean? Like he was waitin' for somethin' to happen. I'd keep a real close watch on him if I were you."

Lew Parker raises himself to his feet.

"Thanks for the information, Logan. I'd better get a move on if I wanna find Sam before I go off duty."

"Good luck, and be careful. You don't want to turn your back on that one for too long; never know what he's got hidin' up his sleeve."

Sheriff Lew Parker tips his Stetson at Lucy.

"Good seein' you, Lucy. Keep your stud on a short leash!"

Lucy looks at Logan with concern etch-ed in her beautiful eyes. Her voice is filled with emotion when she speaks.

"Logan, please promise me that you'll also be careful and watch your back. Everybody knows you and Sam have bad blood between you. I'm asking you; if he provokes you, rather turn around and walk away. Please stay alive and out of jail for my sake."

Logan smiles at Lucy and kisses her.

"I promise I'll look the other way if our paths cross again, honey. You're right of course; he's not worth going to prison for."

Logan and Lucy are enjoying their drinks when someone walks into the restaurant and stops abruptly in the doorway. Because this interrupts their conversation, both look up and are stunned when they recognize the other man.

The man has taken a threatening stance; legs apart and thumbs hooked into his gun belt.

"Lucy, I'd like to speak to you."

Lucy is visibly shocked at this request and looks at Logan with wide eyes. Her voice is unsteady when she talks.

"Ah ... Sam, I don't think that's such a good idea. Besides, I have nothing to discuss with you."

"Why is that, Lucy; 'cause of your boyfriend sittin' next to you? I ain't scared o' him, an' I ain't gonna hurt you none!"

Sam's voice has risen a notch. He points his index finger at Lucy. Lucy's spunk returns; she is over the initial shock.

"Sam Cohen, I'll stick that finger where it doesn't belong, you hear me? Keep your insults to yourself! I've asked Logan to ignore you, but if you came here looking for trouble, I'll be damn sure to ask him to give you a whipping you'll never forget! Now please remove yourself in front of my eyes; the sight of you sickens me!"

"This ain't over by a long shot, Logan. Just you wait an' see. Your turn'll come sooner than you expect!"

Logan and Lucy look at each other, too stunned to reply immediately. When they turn their gaze back to the door, Sam is gone. Logan pulls his shoulders up and they finish their drinks. Leaving the restaurant, they go up to Logan's hotel room.

Sunrise; the following morning.

Sheriff Lew Parker is sitting behind his desk, his chair tilted backward and his feet stretched out on top of his desk. He is twirling a pen around between his fingers, his thoughts occupied with his fruitless search for Sam Cohen last night.

He knows, from previous run-ins with Sam, that he's in town to cause trouble. He arrests the latter almost every time he's in town. Sam can't handle his alcohol. He'll draw his six-gun and threaten to shoot someone, or just shoot up the saloon for the sheer fun of it, endangering everybody's lives.

With a deep sigh, Lew gets to his feet and walks to where the coffeepot is simmering. The fresh aroma of strong coffee filled the office, and Lew fills his tin cup to the brim with the scalding-hot liquid. Carefully sipping the liquid, Lew smacks his lips. The coffee is very tasteful and refreshing. Walking back to his chair, Lew lets his gaze roam the street and boardwalks outside.

He freezes for an instant. Then he hurries to the office door and flings it open. Lew calls out.

"Cohen; step into my office!"

Sam is on his way to the Livery when Lew calls him. Hesitating for a brief moment, he mutters obscenities under his breath before changing direction to the Sheriff's office. Sam enters without knocking and finds himself staring down the barrel of a six-gun.

"Whoa! What the hell ...? Lew, what you pull a gun on me for? That ain't neighbourly!"

"Just take it easy, Sam, and keep them hands where I can see 'em. I know about the beatin' Frank suffered because o' you an' three o' your ranch hands. I been lookin' for you for four days now, Sam. Be a good citizen and tell me what the story is with Frank, an' don't try an' bullshit me. Sit yourself down an' start talkin."

Sam is about to begin with his version of the assault on Frank when someone else enters the office. Lew looks up and Sam turns around in his chair. Sam's face turns pale, while Lew welcomes the visitor.

"Hey, come on in Logan. Sam here was just about to tell me why him an' his men gave Frank such a beatin'. You can corroborate his story, seein' as you were there. Do you mind, Sam?"

Logan is just as surprised to see Sam in the Sheriff's office.

"Well, well, isn't this coincidental after last night, Sam? I hope he told you what happened last night, Lew."

Lew holsters his sidearm and sits back, looking from Sam to Logan. He has a deep furrow between his eyes as he looks at Sam and puts a question to him.

"Last night? What happened last night, Sam; and where?"

There is a long silence after this question of Lew's. Sam opens his mouth to speak but thinks better of it. He stares at the ground, gritting his teeth. Lew turns his attention to Logan.

"Well Logan, seein' as how Sam's tongue's been cut out an' he can't speak, I'm gonna ask you to tell me. What happened last night?"

"Remember you found Lucy an' me in the Hotel restaurant around six o' clock last night while you were lookin' for Sam here? Well, just after you left, this here mister comes waltzing in and demands to speak to Lucy. He insults an' threatens me, an' then just leaves."

"You goin' around threatenin' people now, Sam? When'd you stoop to that level?"

Sam raises his head, once again gritting his teeth and turning crimson-red in his face. His eyes spit fire when he speaks to Lew.

"Lew, all I wanted was to speak to Lucy. Where's the harm in that? I have just as much right to talk to her as anybody else has! I didn't commit no crime!"

Lew shakes his head.

"No Sam, it ain't no crime to talk to anybody, but people can find it offensive when you're rude and demanding."

Lew turns his eyes to Logan.

"What'd Sam here say to you?"

"Well, he said that I would be gettin' my day too and that it would be sooner than I expected. Those were his exact words."

Sheriff Parker's tone is cold and calculated as he addresses Sam.

"Now listen here Sam, and listen good, coz I'm only goin' to say this once. I don't even wanna hear your version of the assault on Frank, coz I know you're goin' to tell me a heap o' bull twang! Turn around an' saddle your pony, then you get the hell out o' town if you don't wanna spend time in the slammer! An' don't lemme see you around town for quite some time, you hear me? Get movin'!"

Sam slowly gets to his feet, a superficial smile on his lips. Without looking in Lew's direction, Sam stops in front of Logan and talks very softly, placing his mouth close to Logan's ear.

"Remember what I said, Prescott. Keep one eye open when you sleep, an' watch your back."

"Cohen! If I ..."

"Relax, Sheriff. Keep your pants on; I'm leavin'."

Logan smiles as he holds Sam's stare before the latter walks out into the hot morning sun.

Sheriff Parker gets up and walks to the window. Both men watch Sam as he walks across the street and enters the Livery. Lew rubs his chin.

"Sam's a real son-of-a-gun! You know that, don't you, Logan? I wouldn't take his warnings lightly if I were you, coz I'll bet a wager that he'll see you dead for humiliatin' him the way you just did."

Logan pulls a face.

"You reckon he has the balls to try somethin' like that, Lew? I know him to be a coward, an' his bark's worse than his bite; I ain't afraid of his threats. He's the kind who'll bushwhack you and walk around telling people that he outdrew you squarely in a gunfight."

They are still standing at Lew's office window. Lew grunts as a horseman comes into sight, exiting the Livery.

"Damn, I'm glad to see him leave town! You just remember, Logan; the tamest dogs have the worst bite. An' watch Lucy's back for her, will you? I'm sure she'll give Sam a run for his money if he tries somethin', but you never know. He has a dirty streak in him."

Logan seconds this statement of Lew.

"Yeah, I'm with you on that one. Lucy's a real darling, but she can stand her ground against any man. My sympathy to anyone who tries to take her on. Ask me; I'm talkin' from experience!"

Both men laugh at this remark from Logan. Lew is first to speak, waving away Logan's comment.

"Yeah, poor you! She might be able to stand her ground, but I think every youngster in the territory wishes they were you. Can I pour you some coffee?"

Logan stands up and heads for the door, shaking his head.

"Naw, thanks Lew; had me a cup just before I came over here. Enjoy the rest o' your weekend; me an' Lucy don't plan on goin' out o' the Hotel room much. I'll see you sometime later during the week before I head back out to my ranch. I'm takin' ole Frank with me; reckon he'll be better off out of town, maybe get his life back together if he has a job. There's enough work on the ranch to keep his mind off o' the alcohol."

Lew rises and walks with Logan to the door. He opens it.

"That's a mighty nice gesture from your side. I hope you're not about to waste your time with gettin' Frank in shape."

Logan shrugs his shoulders.

"That's a chance I'm willin' to take, Lew. See you later."

Lew's gaze follows Logan as he crosses the street to the Hotel, wishing that there were more citizens in Crystal Valley who had just a few of Logan's characteristics. That would make his life as Sheriff so much easier.

CHAPTER SIX

It's late Saturday afternoon in Logan's Hotel room. Logan finds Lucy looking down at him as he awakes from a restful sleep. She smiles as she looks into his eyes.

"Hey there; you awake?"

Logan yawns and stretches his body, at the same time rubbing sleep from his eyes.

"Yeah, I was awake earlier on, but you were still asleep, so I dozed off again. Didn't want to disturb you. Do you feel like goin' to the dancehall tonight; show these townspeople how to dance?"

Lucy makes a face, wrinkling her nose as she does so.

"Why not? I haven't had a night out on the town in quite some time. That would be very relaxing, thank you, Logan."

Logan smiles up at her.

"Good, then it's settled. I'm glad you're looking forward to it. Can't remember when last we had us a good time. Let's go down and have an early dinner before we get dressed to go out."

xxx

Monday morning, 06h15AM; the Circle Double-L ranch.

Although dawn is just breaking over the horizon, the day is already scorching hot. Mike Fuller calls his ranch hands together to issue instructions for the day. Logan will be back in two days, and Mike wants everything on the ranch running smoothly so the crew can be at least halfway with the construction of the house.

"C'mon, get a move on, boys. We have a lot to do before the boss gets back on Wednesday. You know he ain't gonna cuss or anythin' like

45

that, but we talked 'bout surprisin' him, did'n we? Now let's discuss what's in store for us today."

The thundering sound of fast approaching, pounding hooves interrupts their conversation. All the ranch hands, including Mike, are caught off guard, as everyone have left their firearms in the bunkhouse.

Ten horsemen rein their mounts in close to the group of men with six-guns drawn and blazing, firing shots into the air. Riding point is Sam. Mike stares up at Sam, shielding his eyes against the glare of the sun with a raised hand.

"What you doin' here, Cohen? Logan's in town; he'll only be back on Wednesday. You wanna leave a message?"

Sam hosts a smirk on his face and laughs sarcastically. The men who are riding with him, join in.

"It ain't none of your business what I want here, Fuller, but I'll tell you anyhow. I know Logan's in town, see; that's exactly why me an' my men are payin' you a visit. I see there's been quite a bit of progress here. Well, after today Logan'll be back to square one with nothin'!"

Sam's voice rises a notch or two. There's a wild look in his eyes.

"You an' your men have five minutes to get your asses off this land before I shoot you!"

Mike doesn't back down as he holds Sam's stare.

"Go to hell, Cohen! I don't take orders from the likes o' you. You'd really shoot unarmed men? You're a bigger coward than I always imagined! Logan's goin' to kick your ass from here to kingdom come, so no matter what you do today, your days are numbered! Do what you like, I ain't runnin'!"

There is corroboration from the five other ranch hands at this statement from Mike. Sam throws his head back and laughs, then spits at Mike.

"Well, ain't no-one can say I didn't give you fair warnin'. You think you're brave; I call it stupidity! I admire it, though. Say your last prayers, 'cause you're 'bout to meet your maker!"

There is a moment of confusion as Mike storms the semi-circle of men holding them at gunpoint. The other ranch hands are on his heels. A single gunshot sounds, the echo reverberating across the open landscape. The impact of the bullet flings Mike back and spins him around. It takes him high on the left side of his upper torso.

A volley of gunshots from Sam's group of men follows and carefully placed shots find their marks amongst the five remaining ranch hands. They fall like axed trees, life spilling from them as their blood turns the ground a deep crimson red. Sam holds up his hand.

"That's enough, men. You're only wastin' ammunition now. There ain't nobody left to tell tales. Let's get to work!"

The bunkhouse is set alight, as are the few wooden frames that make up the outside construction of the ranch house.

Sam instructs four of his men to round up the cattle and take them to the free ranging land on Sam's ranch.

"We'll brand the cattle there later this afternoon. See that two of you get the fire goin' so long!"

The Double-D ranch, sunset.

Dan Walker enjoys his Whisky, while Brenda Walker nurses a long-stemmed glass of red wine. Lucy never uses any strong alcohol, and enjoys some freshly squeezed orange juice. The sun has just set behind the horizon when Lucy becomes aware of five horsemen approaching the ranch house, but they're still too far-off to discern their facial features.

"Are you expecting anybody, daddy? It's rather late to be riding around, and it doesn't look like any of your workers."

Dan shakes his head, a deep frown creasing his forehead.

"No, honey. I wonder who in blazes this is. Can't think of anybody I'd want to see at this time of day. Well, let's wait until they get here; that's all we can do. Maybe they're lost or something. Go on inside and bring us some cold water; they might be thirsty."

Without any further ado Lucy gets up and enters the house. She's pouring water from a container in the fridge when she hears her mother scream, followed by the unmistakable sound of a high caliber rifle shot. Lucy runs to her father's study, where they keep all the rifles and handguns.

Through the window of the study Lucy can make out the features of two of the riders. She gasps involuntarily at the sight of one of them. Lucy grabs a Winchester Carbine from the rifle rack and runs to the patio door. Taking cover behind a huge pillar, Lucy takes aim and fires off two rapid shots.

Her bullets find their intended targets and knock two men from their saddles. The remaining three men return fire, their shots drilling holes in the pillar and showering plaster over Lucy. Lucy's mother, who has been crouching in her chair, sees her chance and raises herself. She runs for the patio door's entrance. Brenda manages to run a couple of feet before two bullets drill into her back, hurling her forward.

Lucy opens fire again in the hope of hitting another one of the intruders. The men hastily flee the scene. Lucy runs to her mother and kneels at her side, cradling her head in her arms. Brenda's breath is shallow and uneven, and blood is frothing on her lips. She tries to speak, but her voice falters and her eyes roll back. Her eyes turn glassy, and her body shudders as she exhales a last painful breath.

Lucy is beside herself with heartache. She looks to where her father is lying. Sam has shot Dan at close range with a shotgun, and ripped his chest cavity wide open, killing him instantly. Lucy sits on the patio for quite some time. She is too shocked to think clearly, but she knows that she has to get away from the ranch. The attackers know that she is still alive, and Lucy knows without a doubt that they will be coming back to finish her off.

Lucy covers both her parents with sheets before saddling her horse. Taking a saddlebag filled with ammunition for both her handgun and rifle, she sets off toward town. The only person she can think of in this time of crisis, is Logan. He'll know what to do.

THE WOUNDED MAN IS holding them back. He falls behind and slumps forward in his saddle. Sam is furious. Two of his men are dead and one seriously wounded. He was under the impression that Lucy is still in town with Logan, because he didn't see her pass his ranch. Damn! Sam turns on the remaining member of his men, who is sitting astride his horse next to Sam.

"What the hell you waitin' for, Junior; better days? Move your ass and go fetch Cole! Can't you see he's about to drop outta his saddle? You shoulda stayed an' seen to it that woman's dead like I told you to, but no, you were too scared she was goin' to pop you! She damn well nearly did, too. We gotta go back and see she's taken care of before she spills the beans. I know her; she ain't goin' to hang around very long. Take Cole back to the ranch an' meet me here again. Come on; move your fat ass before I put a bullet in it!"

Junior whips his horse with the reins and gallops to where Cole's horse has halted. Cole is clinging to the saddle-horn to keep him from falling off. Junior takes the reins of Cole's horse and at a fast trot, leads the way to Sam's ranch. Sam doesn't have to wait long for Junior's return. Together they head for the Walker ranch.

Sam immediately sees that there is no one home. The corpses of the two elderly ranchers still lay where they had fallen earlier.

"Hey, Junior; go inside the house an' see if you can find any kerosene or somethin' similar, somethin' that'll burn. If you do, spill it all over. I'll keep watch in case someone comes snoopin.'"

Junior does as he is told. He knows better than to question Sam and his ways. Junior wants out after this. He's done pretty rotten things in his life up to now, but this is taking it too far. He doesn't have the heart to kill another human being, but he is now an accomplice to two murders. He has decided that he will just pack up his clothes and leave without even asking for his wages.

Sam doesn't have his pocket watch with him, but guesses that it should be around eight o' clock. There is only half a moon, which makes the night dark and ominous. Sam feels on edge and jumps when an Owl hoots not far from him. He is just about to go and see what is keeping Junior, when he hears a loud "whoosh."

The house is ablaze, fiery tongues licking at the dry timber and furniture. Within a couple of minutes the fire is out of control and can be seen for miles. Sam and Junior give their horses free reins. Looking back, Sam is satisfied. There is only one other small problem that needs to be taken care of ...

Crystal Valley: 7h30PM.

The sound of loud hoof beats echo through the quiet town as Lucy enters the main street at full speed. She pulls back on the reins so violently that her horse rears up on its hind legs, nearly throwing her in the process.

Lucy is still in a state of shock when she dismounts her horse and stumbles through the Hotel's front door into the foyer. Her legs give way and she falls onto her knees, raw sobs tearing from her. The nightshift clerk has already called Logan in his room on the telephone, and rushes to help Lucy to her feet.

The clerk helps Lucy to a chair. Lucy looks bewildered, her eyes filled with anxiety. She tries to speak, but words escape her. She looks at the staircase and sees Logan rushing down the stairs two at a time. In a flash Logan is kneeling beside her, encircling her in his arms. He feels her body tremble. Lucy's voice is shaking when she speaks through her tears.

"Logan! I'm so glad you're here! Some... something terrible happened at our ranch earlier tonight!"

Lucy breaks down again. Logan comforts her until she becomes calm.

"That's alright, baby; take your time. Whatever it is, I'll be with you every step o' the way, Lucy."

Lucy at last takes control of herself again. She gets up and walks to the large window overlooking the main street. She faces the street for a couple of seconds before turning around, her hands clenched together. Looking at Lucy, Logan can't believe that it's the same person he comforted a few minutes ago. Her eyes have a glint of steel to them, and her voice is cold.

"Five gunmen came to our ranch earlier tonight, Logan. On their way in daddy sent me inside for a pitcher of water, under the impression that these men were visitors. I went inside to fetch the water when I heard gunfire. Looking through the dining-room window, I saw them shoot my parents! I recognized Sam as one of the shooters, Logan! They were going to shoot me as well, because Sam told his men to go inside the house and see that I'm taken care of. I returned fire, killing one of his men and wounding another. Sam and the other intruder fled and I raced here to get to you. I'm going to kill Sam, Logan, and he's going to suffer for a long time before he dies!"

Lucy's breathing becomes more rapid, and she clenches her fists as she grits on her teeth. Logan is about to walk to Lucy when she raises her hands and indicates for him to stay put.

"Don't come any closer, Logan. I don't want to be crowded now. You being here is all I need for the moment; it's enough."

For a moment the hurt lies shallow and raw in Lucy's eyes. Logan's heart bleeds at the sight of Lucy's hurt.

"I understand, Lucy, but just know that I'm here when you need me. Like I said; I'm with you every step of the way."

"Thank you, Logan. Would you please escort me back to our ranch tomorrow morning? I have to get my parents brought to town by the undertaker's."

Logan nods his head.

"Yes, of course I will. We can go to the undertaker's together. I also want to go and have a look at what's been going on at my ranch while I've been gone. In the meantime, let's get you to my room and into bed. Would you like me to get Doctor Ford to come over and give you something so you can have a peaceful night's rest?"

Lucy hesitates for a moment before shaking her head in denial.

"No thank you, Logan; I'll be alright. I know you mean well, but you also know that I'm not fond of taking medicine. I just want to take a hot bath before going to bed."

Logan had taken Lucy to his hotel-room while talking to her, and he now points to the bathroom.

"It's yours for as long as you like, Lucy. I'll go and take care of your horse; see that she's stabled and fed for the night. When I return, you should be finished."

Logan kisses her on the cheek and leaves the room.

As the water closes around Lucy's body where she lies back in the bath, soaking in the rich fragrance of the foam–bath, she finds it hard to believe that she will never again see her parents, hear their laughter or hug them.

The hot water has a calming effect on her, and Lucy thinks back to what her mother always used to say. Her mother believed that water has healing powers. It appears she was right all along, after all. Lucy smiles softly and her eyes turn watery. She quickly checks herself.

"I have to stay strong now and not go weak", Lucy thinks out loud. As she gets out of the bath, she hears Logan enter the room. He calls out to Lucy.

"I'm back, honey. I'll just sit down on the bed and wait for you."

XXX

Sunrise: the following morning.

Logan and Lucy are on their way to the Double Diamond ranch with an entourage following behind them. They smell the stench of burnt wood from some distance, and small plumes of dark smoke are visible from afar. Lucy utters a sound of alarm and urges her horse forward.

Logan tries to take hold of her horses' reins to hold it back, but Lucy foresees his plan and pulls the reins to her left, moving out of Logan's reach. Lucy halts her horse and dismounts before Logan can get to her.

Destruction is not the word. The once beautiful house is burnt to the ground, some of the wood still smoldering.

The fire consumed the bodies of Lucy's parents and they're burnt beyond recognition. Lucy sinks to her knees and cries for a long time, while Logan holds his distance. At last she pulls herself up and walks to where Logan is standing. Her voice is bitter when she speaks.

"This is it, Logan! It was bad enough killing them, but this? They never caused any living being any harm, so why do this?"

Logan conceals his seething anger and pretends to be calm and collective.

"This is the work of a coward, Lucy. You said last night that you recognized Sam as one of them, so let's go to my ranch and gather a few of my men before we ride out to Sam's place for a show-down."

Lucy stares at Logan and turns to the undertaker who comes closer.

"Please take my parents to the morgue. I'll come by later to discuss the funeral with you."

She turns back to Logan.

"Let's go."

xxx

It's clear to Logan as he and Lucy get closer to his ranch, that something is not right. They are a quarter of a mile away when Logan's keen eyesight catches movement some distance ahead of them. Bringing his binoculars up, Logan trains it on the spot where he can see the movement. What he sees makes him cringe.

Vultures? This early in the morning on his land? Logan points it out to Lucy, who answers that she has seen it. Logan puts spurs to his horse with Lucy hot on his heels. Neither one of them are prepared for the sight that greets them.

Both Logan and Lucy gag and turn away as the vultures hop a little distance away; waiting ...

Lucy becomes aware that Logan is deathly silent. Looking at him, she notices that his face is chalk-white with shock. Before Lucy can think of something to say Logan's demeanor changes. He grits his teeth so hard that Lucy thinks he might break some teeth. The muscles along his jawbone bulge with the strain.

Then Logan screams. Lucy has never before experienced this side of Logan's character, and it scares her. She has always known him to be calm and collected; sure of himself and what he does.

Logan draws his six-gun and empties it into the air before holstering it again. His eyes spit death when he finally looks up and meets Lucy's stare.

"They'll pray that they were never born. This is our land; they wrecked the house I was building for us, stole my cattle and shot the men who protected our land. Everything's ruined; they're as good as dead!"

Lucy knows she has to say something.

"Who do you think could have done something so awful, Logan? I mean ..."

"I'll bet my life this is Sam! Couldn't get me outta the way, so he thought he'd teach me a lesson where it hurts most."

"You really think he'd go this far?"

Logan nods his head affirmatively.

"Yeah, I do, but this time he's chewed off too much. We have to go an' tell Lew what's happened', just so he knows it ain't us breakin' the law here. But first things first; Sam's ranch is on our way to town, so we'll make a stop there first an' hear what he has to say for himself. I stake my life on the fact that he's goin' to deny everythin'. Come what may, of one thing you can be sure, an' that's that I'm goin' to kill Sam Cohen! He's caused enough trouble an' heartache. Let's go see him."

xxx

Logan and Lucy rein their mounts in behind some large boulders on the crest of a hilltop overlooking Sam's ranch about half a mile away. Both remove their binoculars from their saddlebags and start scouring the land stretched out before them. Everything is peaceful and quiet; too peaceful to Logan's liking.

"I don't like the way things look down there, Lucy. Everythin's just a mite too quiet. Seems like he's suspectin' someone to show up, or somethin' to happen. Let's ride a mile or so to the West and approach from another direction."

Lucy is all for it.

"Yes, that sounds like a plan to me. Come on, let's go!"

After a quick twenty-minute ride, they are at the exact spot where Logan wants to be.

Some distance off there is movement under a clump of trees and pointing to it, Logan urges his horse forward with soft clicking sounds. Logan and Lucy are almost there, when one in the group of men looks up and sees them approaching. He immediately makes alarm.

Seven men are grouped together under the trees, including Sam. A fire is burning, and several young steers and cows are fenced in behind a makeshift camp close by. Logan can tell at a quick glance that they are branding the cattle. The men are all wearing their chaps and thick leather gloves.

Sam steps forward and spits on the ground.

"What you doin' on my land, Prescott; you an' that pretty little missy o' yours? You're trespassin' on private property, an' you damn well know I can shoot you for that! I have six witnesses present who can testify to that, don't I, boys?"

Sam's ranch hands corroborate this by nodding their heads. Sam grins, and spits tobacco again.

"You look a little yellow now, Prescott. Not as brave as the other day in the saloon, now are we? Oh yeah, don't forget the incident in Lew's office. I've a good mind to shoot you right off your horse!"

Logan changes the subject. He nods with his head in the direction of the cattle.

"You boys doing some branding, I see. Where'd you buy these cattle from, Sam, 'cause a few of them look pretty familiar to me. My men are dead an' my house destroyed. My cattle are gone. Know anythin' about it?"

The six men look at one another and when they realize the implication of Logan's question, go for their guns. Sam's voice stops them.

"Take it easy, boys. Now Logan, if I understand your question, you're implying that I killed your men and torched your house before stealing all your cattle. Is that right? That's a pretty nasty thing to do, an' even worse to accuse me!"

"Well Sam, from where I'm sittin', I can clearly see my brand on one o' those steers. It's easy to change my brand to that of yours, and yes, I'm sayin' that you're responsible for what happened at my ranch. As a matter of fact, you're also responsible for killin' Lucy's parents last night. She recognized you. We're on our way to Lew now, an' you can bet your sorry ass we'll be comin' back with him. You've gone too far this time, Cohen!"

Logan starts backing up his horse and takes Lucy's by the reins. Sam's facial expression expresses his intense dislike for Logan. The latter sees the raw hatred burning in Sam's stare as he steps forward. His lips curl upward menacingly.

There is no time for Logan to react, Sam's hand streaks down with uncanny speed, drawing his six-gun from its holster. He is firing as his arm comes up. Logan draws his gun when the first bullet smashes into his right upper torso, flinging him sideways and from the saddle. Logan's shot goes wild, thumping into a tree-trunk close by.

The searing hot pain makes Logan gasp for breath. He looks up, trying to find Lucy. She has pulled her Winchester carbine from its sheath tied to her saddle, and is firing at the group of men. Two men stumble and fall to the ground. The rest scatter for cover.

Logan tries to call out to her to make a run for it, but the words come out in a hoarse whisper. Logan brings his arm up and waves at Lucy, when another bullet hits him in his side. He loses consciousness, aware only of the overbearing pain.

Lucy tries to get to Logan so she can get him out of the line of fire, but the shooting has become so intense that she has to turn her horse and run. She has gone a hundred meters or so when she hears the unmistakable crack of a heavy caliber rifle, and then the 'thump' as the bullet finds its target in the small of her back.

The impact of the heavy-grain bullet nearly succeeds in knocking Lucy from her saddle, but she clings with brute strength. She grits on her teeth and lies forward in the saddle. Lucy knows she's in trouble, and swings her horse in the direction of town.

CHAPTER SEVEN

Sheriff Lew Parker is sitting behind his desk, his brain wrapped around a very unpleasant thought. He scowls. It just never seems to end. It's as if evil has come to settle in this once peaceful town.

Sheriff Parker can't concentrate on his work this morning. He has heard some news in town this morning concerning Lucy's well-being, as well as that of her parents. As Sheriff of the town, it's his duty to follow up on complaints of a serious matter, but he hasn't seen Lucy around town.

Asking around, he discovers that Logan has left with Lucy, and feels more at ease. If there is anyone who can resolve Lucy's problems, it's Logan. Lew hears the sound of a buckboard's wheels rolling into town and looks up. He recognizes Iziah Tanner, the town Mortician.

There's something on the back of the buckboard covered by a tarpaulin. Lew knows that it has to be a dead body, gets up and walks over to the morgue to see who it is.

Lew arrives at the morgue almost the same time as the buckboard. He walks straight to where Iziah is busy.

"Who do you have here, Iziah? I didn't see you go out this mornin.'"

Iziah doesn't pay much attention to Lew. He mumbles to himself before looking at Lew.

"I'll come around to your office to see you in a coupla minutes, Sheriff. Tell you what I know as soon's I get there."

Twenty minutes later Iziah shoves his face around the doorpost of the Sheriff's office.

"Howdy, Sheriff. You wanted to see me?"

Sheriff Lew Parker kicks a chair out from under his desk.

"Sit down, Iziah. Yeah, like I asked you back there at the morgue; who did you bring in on the back of your wagon?"

Iziah's forehead creases as he frowns.

"Well hell, I thought you knew. That there's Lucy's parents. Shot last night by five gunmen on their ranch without any warnin'. As I understand it, Lucy returned fire; wounded one, killed another. Then she came here lookin' for Logan last night. When we got to Lucy's ranch this mornin', we found the place'd been torched; her parents too. That's it, man."

Lew Parker can't believe what Iziah has told him. Lucy's parents are well known and loved around these parts. The shock has him speechless and stunned for a minute.

"Wait a minute ...; what the hell?! Did she say who shot her parents? People can't just come into my territory and go on a shooting spree!"

"Yeah, Lucy did say, but I can't recall the name. You'll have to ask her when she gets back. I reckon she'll be by later today. Just keep an eye out for her."

Lew is frustrated beyond words. Iziah hasn't told him anything of significant value that he could use. He'd have to be patient and wait it out. Then a thought strikes Lew. Maybe he should take a ride out to the Double Diamond and see if he can find anything substantial to work with while he waits for Lucy to return.

Lew rushes out of the office, putting his Stet-son on as he closes the office door behind him. He crosses the street and enters the Livery, quickly saddling his Pinto. Lew leaves town at a fast gallop.

Early afternoon.

The sun rides hot and high. Lucy's mare runs to where the trail starts that leads to town. Along the trail Lucy briefly regains consciousness, and steers her horse towards a thicket of dense brush. If Sam and his men decide to follow her, she will be unnoticeable from the trail.

Her horse eats of the tall sweet grass for a while before returning to the trail by itself and heading for town. Before long, Lucy's unconscious body slips sideways from the saddle and falls into the tall grass that grows along the trail.

Lucy's horse stops and returns to where Lucy is lying, bending its elegant neck to pull at her clothing with its lips. There's no response from Lucy. Her mare nudges her softly on the shoulder with its muzzle and whinnies.

It's at this minute that Lew rounds a bend in the trail and hears the whinnying before seeing the horse a hundred yards or so in front of him. It appears to Lew as if the animal is in distress. Lew recognizes the horse as that of Lucy's and notices that it's busy with something in the tall grass.

Lew reins in and dismounts. He is shocked at the sight that greets him. Lucy is lying on her stomach, a trickle of blood still running from the wound in the small of her back.

Careful not to cause Lucy any more harm, Lew picks her up and lifts her in an upright position onto his saddle, also mounting to sit behind Lucy. Riding double is the only way he can get Lucy to the doctor in town.

Without any further ado, Lew turns his horse around and at a fast gallop, heads for town.

SAM SNIGGERS LIKE A Hyena as he sees the bullet smack into Lucy's back. He can imagine the excruciating pain that bullet must cause. By his estimate, Lucy won't live long; well, not long enough to tell anybody what has happened, anyway. His stare focuses on Logan for a moment. There is no movement, and Sam gives himself a pat on the back.

Thinking back, he has to admit that he was shaken by the precise manner in which Logan portrayed the events leading to their confrontation. Come to think of it, Logan has always been too damn smart for his own good. It's auspicious that there will be no more meddling from him. Sam smiles, but it lacks emotion.

Lucy has shot up two of his men pretty bad. They're still alive, but only just. Lucy is an excellent markswoman. Sam calls for his men.

"C'mon boys, gather your things an' let's get goin'. We can carry on with the brandin' tomorrow. We've done enough for one day."

One of Sam's men, a Mexican, comments on their situation.

"That lady messed us up pretty bad, Sam. What we gonna do with Charlie and Reno; they can't even get up off the ground."

Sam ponders on this for a moment, and subsequently nods his head.

"Yeah, you're right, Pedro. They ain't no use to us. They have to get medical help first, an' that's gonna cause unnecessary questions from the law; somethin' I can do without. Gonna cost me money too."

Without as much as flinching, Sam draws his six-gun and fires off two quick rounds. The two wounded men die without knowing it.

"C'mon, I ain't tellin' you again; pack up and let's go! You wanna join your friends? Just speak the words an' I'll be happy to oblige."

There is a quick exchange of looks between the remaining three men before they hurriedly kill the fire and pack the tools before mounting their horses. Without a second glance at Logan's lifeless figure, the four men leave the campsite at a fast gallop.

It's quiet for a long time while the sun burns down mercilessly from a powder-blue sky. Then, high in the sky, a tiny speck appears, followed by another and another. The specks draw closer, circling lower with each turn.

After what seems like an eternity, there is but the slightest movement from Logan. He feels delirious from pain, and each movement makes him wince, gasping for breath. The bullet wounds have stopped bleeding, making thick crusts of blood in his side and on his chest.

The first buzzards land a few feet away, and stare at Logan with hungry eyes, flapping their wings and hopping around in anticipation of a feast. When Logan moves and utters a low groaning sound, the largest of the Vultures screeches and moves away from Logan.

Logan crawls laboriously into the welcoming shade of long branches. He was in the scorching sun for some time, and had burnt blisters in his face and neck. In an agonizing attempt, Logan pulls himself into a sitting position against a tree trunk. He grits on his teeth and has to fight against darkness trying to overwhelm him.

Time means nothing to Logan as he lies there, slipping in and out of consciousness. Far-off and faintly he hears the whinnying of a horse. Darkness closes around him as he strains his ears to listen ...

Doctor Ford is battling to cope with both his patients at the same time. They are both in serious condition and to worsen the situation, they're unconscious and have lost a lot of blood.

"What do you think, Doc; will you be able to pull them through? Whoever did this has to be caught, and I can't do anythin' unless I know who it is."

"Well, it's difficult to say, Sheriff. They're both shot up pretty bad and in serious condition. They've lost a lot of blood. I can't even try and remove the bullet from Lucy's back, coz I don't know how close it is to the spine. I can just hope that it didn't cause any irreversible damage."

"When will we know if they have a chance of surviving the odds?"

Doctor Ford pulls his shoulders up, shaking his head.

"We'll have to wait and see, Lew. I'd say forty-eight to seventy-two hours. It can go either way."

"Alright, then I'll just have to wait, I suppose. If there's any change in either one's condition, let me know."

"I will. In the meantime there's another patient I have to see to."

The Sheriff stops short in his tracks.

"Oh yeah, I almost forgot; how's old Frank doin'? Gotta have a talk with him as well when he feels up to it. Lemme know when he's good an' ready."

"Frank's doing pretty good. I must say, he recovered rather quickly for someone his age after the beating he took. I wouldn't be surprised if Sam's to blame for Logan and Lucy too."

"Yeah, me neither. Provin' it's the hard part. Be seein' you, Doc; I have some business to take care of."

xxx

Lew Parker rides down the dirt road leading to Sam Cohen's house. He's alert, because Sam is a loose cannon; very unpredictable. Lew is sure that he is being watched at this exact minute through the lenses of a pair of binoculars. He has goosebumps.

Lew pulls back on the reins of his mount a few feet from the wide porch that runs along the entire one side of the house. There's no sign of life.

"Put your hands where I can see 'em Lawman, an' don't make any sudden moves if you value your life!"

This order comes so abruptly that Lew jerks involuntarily and yanks out his six-gun. The appearance of Sam from around the side of the house holding a Winchester trained on him, restrains any further movement from Lew. Sam smiles sarcastically.

"Shoe's on the other foot now, ain't it, Lew? You feelin' a little threatened now? Speak up; don't just sit there gawkin' at me!"

Sam's tone changes from sarcastic to agitated.

"Simmer down, Sam. I ain't here to cause trouble. Just wanna ask you a couple o' questions."

"Regardin' what? I don't owe you or anybody else any explanation! Ask what you came here to ask and get the hell off my land, before I shoot you for trespassin'!"

"You look a bit tense, Sam. Why? Alright, here goes. Where were you yesterday, and also the day before? There're a couple o' incidents I'm lookin' into that need some explainin'."

Sam 's smile is cold.

"Well, that's easy. I was right here. You can ask any of my men; they'll back my story. I been home since Saturday after our little tangle in your office. Why d'you ask; anythin' of importance happen?"

Lew stares at the man standing before him. Did he imagine it, or is there a little flicker of fear in his eyes?

"Yeah, as a matter of fact, somethin' did happen. Two people were shot an' killed out in the open. Found 'em purely by luck, an' now I have two murders to solve. Reason why I'm askin' is you an' Logan had a fallin'-out last Friday night. He's one o' the two dead people. The other's Lucy. Found her shot in the back with a heavy caliber rifle. Looks like the work of a bushwhacker. Lucy's a very good shot. I had a look at her rifle, an' it was fired, okay. If I find someone with a bullet in him, I'll know who the killer is. Your men all accounted for, Sam?"

"My men are all accounted for, Lew. You mean to tell me that Logan and Lucy have been shot? Who'd do such a thing? That's just nasty! I hope you catch the killer, or killers, for that matter. There somethin' else you wanna know?"

Lew Parker shakes his head.

"Naw. Just know this; if I find out that either you or any of your men had somethin' to do with this, I'll personally come for you. It ain't a threat; it's a friendly warnin'. So if there's somethin' you wanna tell me, now's your chance."

For a split second it seems like Sam is about to say something. His mouth opens and closes, before he casts his eyes down and mumbles incoherent words. Then he recovers and looks up at Lew.

"I told you; I was here all the time; I dunno a damn thing! Now get the hell off o' my ranch, an' don't come back or you'll be sorry!"

Lew and Sam stare at one another for a few seconds before Lew starts backing his horse away.

"Alright, Sam; I'll go."

Lew turns his horse and without a backward glance, leaves the ranch at a fast gallop.

xxx

Sam watches the Sheriff gallop away, then turns around and walks towards the bunkhouse.

"Pedro, Danny; come here!"

The two men appear from the bunkhouse and saunter to where Sam is standing. Pedro is the first to speak.

"You called us, Sam? What you want us to do for you?"

"I want you two to get rid of those bodies. Bury them deep; I don't want them found; ever! Is that understood?"

The two men bob their heads to indicate that they have heard.

"Good. Now get goin', an' don't let anybody see you. I don't trust that Sheriff. He might still be hangin' around."

XXX

It's been two weeks since Lew went to see Sam on his ranch regarding the shooting on Logan and Lucy. Lew hopes that he will see the latter in town some time or other after the incident, but alas; there is no sighting nor word from him or any of his men.

Logan's condition worsens two days after the shooting. He becomes delirious with fever, and although unconscious and unaware of his surroundings, tries to speak out. Lew however, can't hear what Logan is saying, as his speech is incoherent. He prods Doctor Ford about this.

"Doc, do you reckon he'll come out of this condition if you manage to break his fever?"

"He might, Lew. Like I said, we'll have to wait it out. I removed the bullet from his side, but couldn't take a chance with the bullet that entered his chest area. Too close to the heart. He'll most probably have to walk with it lodged in there somewhere if he pulls through, until the day he dies."

"How's Lucy doin'; she still holdin' up?"

Doctor Ford bobs his head.

"She's a strong one, that Lucy. That shot woulda killed plenty a man. She seems mighty determined to cling to life, the way I see it. Lost more'n her share of blood. I'm worried that she might not be able to walk ever again."

Lew's muscles along his jawline tighten as he stares at the quiet figure of Lucy where she lies on her side.

"Wish I could catch the one responsible for shootin' 'em. Then there's the senseless killin' of her parents an' the ranch hands on Logan's ranch. I reckon the same person shot both of 'em and Lucy's parents. I don't know what to make of Logan's ranch hands, though. Don't make no sense to me at all."

67

Doctor Ford scratches the side of his jaw.

"Yes, it's a damn shame Lucy losing her parents that way. Life is unpredictable. And to Lucy ..."

There is movement and then a loud groan emits from Lucy. Her eyelids flutter before she slowly opens them and searches for the voices that reach her.

"Where... where am I?"

Doctor Ford is standing next to her bed and holds her down when she tries to sit up.

"Take it easy, Lucy; you've taken a very bad hit in the back. It's close to your spine, and I don't know what the extent of the damage is. Just lie still for a couple of minutes. I'd like to do a few tests if I may?"

Lucy nods her head affirmatively.

"That's alright, Doc; do what you have to. I'll behave."

"Do you have any pain in your back or legs?"

Lucy shakes her head.

"No, I don't have pain anywhere. Where's Logan? He was shot, and I couldn't do anything to get him out of danger; Lew?"

Lew tries to calm her down.

"There, there, Lucy. Don't worry; Logan's here, but he's still unconscious. He took two bullets, lost a lot of blood. Can you tell me what happened out there, and do you have any suspicion on who shot your parents?"

Lucy looks Lew straight in the eye and again shakes her head.

"Sorry, Sheriff; I have no idea who shot my parents. Logan and me were just riding when someone started shooting at us. Logan took the first bullets. I tried to help him, but couldn't. When I realized that I had to get out of there, I turned my horse and ran for cover. I'd almost reached cover when I felt this searing pain in my back and then the crack of a heavy caliber rifle. I lost consciousness immediately afterwards. How long have I been lying here?"

Lew Parker isn't convinced that Lucy has told him everything, but keeps quiet about it. He answers Lucy's question, however.

"Two weeks, Lucy. You've been unconscious for two weeks. I found you on the trail, and Logan a couple o' hundred yards further down, way off the trail on open range."

Lucy sits up with a shocked expression on her face.

"Two weeks?! I... I have to get going. There're some things I need to take care of."

Lucy swings her feet of the bed and gets up. She sways a little and has to hold onto the bed not to fall. The Sheriff grabs hold of her arm.

"I'm alright, Sheriff; just a little dizzy there for a moment."

"Where you goin'?"

"I'm going to the undertaker's first. Have my parents been put to rest yet, Lew, and where'd you put my horse?"

Lew shakes his head.

"No, they're still lyin' in the mortuary, Lucy. Ben didn't want to do anythin' until he'd spoken to you. Your horse's stabled in the Livery."

There is no further reaction from Lucy. With renewed vivacity she leaves the doctor's rooms and heads for the stables.

SAM CALLS ONE OF HIS ranch hands to execute an order.

"Johnny, come here! Make it quick and don't make me come and fetch you; you'll regret it!"

Johnny Munro is tall and skinny; not a very hard-working ranch hand. Johnny rather delegates than do the work himself. Sam has been watching Johnny for a while now, and is thinking of letting him go.

"You called, Sam?"

"Yeah, I called you. Go down to the stables an' saddle my horse for me; pronto! An' don't tell someone else to do it either. I'm givin' you the instruction; you do it!"

"Yeah, yeah; no need to worry. I'll do it. What you goin' to do in town, anyways? I think that Sheriff's waitin' for you to mess up. Once you do, he's goin' to pounce on you. I'd be careful if I was you."

Sam's stare gives Johnny cold shivers. He knows he has bitten off too much this time when Sam speaks.

"Listen, you piece o' trash; did you hear me ask for your opinion? It ain't none o' your damn business why I'm goin' into town. You work for me, which means I'm the boss, an' you listen when I speak; got that? Men have died for less than that. Get a move on with my horse!"

Sam draws his gun and fires two shots into the ground between Johnny's feet. Johnny turns and runs as fast as his long legs can carry him. Within ten minutes Sam's mount is saddled and ready to go. Sam rides off towards town.

Sam sits at the bar nursing his drink. He's already had a few stiff ones, and can feel that it's impairing his judgement. He tries to focus on the reason for his visit to town, but can't really think of one. He gives up after a while and swallows the Whisky with one gulp. Sam slams the glass down hard on the bar counter.

"Pour me another, Charlie, and keep 'em com-in'. As a matter o' fact; I think I'll take what's left o' the bottle."

Charlie shakes his head in denial.

"Sorry, Sam, you've had enough as it is. Go get yourself a room at the hotel and sleep it off. I ain't givin' you any more liquor."

Muttering obscenities under his breath, Sam staggers through the batwing doors into the chilly night air.

"Damn; it's cold!" Sam mutters.

Holding onto the walkway's timber poles, Sam carefully descends the steps one at a time. He's about to step onto the dirt road when he notices a figure appear from the shadows behind him. Turning, Sam sees the figure bolt towards him. The unknown figure collides violently with Sam, shoving him hard to land spread-eagled in the dirt.

The fall winds Sam for a couple of seconds, and when he sits up and looks about him, there's nothing. The street is ghostly quiet, and yet he can swear ...

"No, that's not possible; she's dead." Sam speaks out loud. He shakes his head, confused at what he's just seen and experienced. Whichever way Sam tries to puzzle it together, he can't wrap his head around it. He is completely sober now and convinced that it isn't his imagination.

"I saw Lucy; I ain't mad! Or maybe, hell, I dunno what to think! Lew told me she was dead, now ..."

Sam's conversation with himself ends abruptly when a kick in his back forces him to double over backwards, screaming in agony. The figure bending over him is wearing a thick, long waistcoat, with a

Stetson pulled down low over the top half of the face. It's impossible to recognize the person.

Suddenly Sam is staring down the muzzle of a very large gun. He sees a flash of orange before the bullet smashes into the second knuckle of his right hand. The bullet makes a hole the size of a dollar coin.

Lights turn on in the Sheriff's office. The figure disappears into the night, leaving Sam disoriented and weak with pain. Doctor Ford arrives on the scene with a carry-bag. After inspecting Sam's hand, Doctor Ford sanitizes it and bandages it up with a thick bandage.

"There you go, Cohen. The injection's for pain. There's nothing more I can do other than that. Just keep it clean and change the bandage twice a day, then you'll be alright. You're going to lose most of the use in that hand, so start getting used to it. Who shot you, Cohen?"

Sam's head sways from side to side, his voice heavy with pain.

"I, I dunno, doc. Just saw a glimpse of a shadow behind me. I got shoved from behind, then kicked in the back. The person who shot me, was dressed in a long trench coat. I couldn't see the face. For a moment there I thought, uhm, that it looked like Lucy Walker, but the Sheriff told me she was dead as a doornail."

Doctor Ford nods his head.

"That she is, Sam. What a nasty affair being shot in the back. I think you should talk to Wesley so he can report tonight's incident to Lew in the morning. He can take it from there."

The nightshift Deputy is present when Sam tells his story to Doctor Ford. Wesley McFarlane helps Sam to his feet and takes him to the Sheriff's office.

XXX

06h00 AM, The following morning.

Lew listens intently to the story his deputy tells him. He can't believe his ears.

"What the hell, Wes? So Sam says he never even saw his attacker? That's strange. Sounds almost like the attacker didn't want himself to be recognized. Where's Sam at the moment?"

Wesley pulls his shoulders up.

"Dunno, Lew. Said he was going over to the Hotel to get himself a room there. He hasn't left the Hotel's far as I can recollect."

Lew Parker is stunned. He doesn't know what to make of the situation. It doesn't sit right with him. Deep in thought, Lew picks his Stetson up from his desk and heads for the door. With his hand on the doorknob, he turns around to his Deputy.

"I'm sorry to ask you, Wes, but will you see if you can find Lucy for me? I know you're tired, but I really need your help with this one. She just upped and left the Doc's rooms yesterday, an' I ain't seen her since. Don't know if she's around town. If you find her, ask her to stay put, an' then you come an' tell me where she's at. Tell no one else, understand? I'm off to see if Sam can tell me anythin' else. Meet me back here in thirty minutes."

Wesley smiles laconically.

"Think nothin' of it, Lew. See you in thirty."

Sam is lying flat on his back in his Hotel room on the bed. He has a bad backache, which restrains him from doing much. Worst of all is his hand. Blood is still seeping through the thick bandage Doctor Ford has wrapped around his hand. Sam didn't sleep at all. The pain is excruciating.

A knock on his door brings him upright and he swings his legs off the bed. It's still early, and he wonders who his visitor can be. Nursing his crushed hand, Sam walks across the room to open the door. Sam isn't surprised to find the Sheriff standing in the hallway.

"Come in, Lew. Don't know what else there is that I can tell you. Told that Deputy of yours everythin' I know. Whoever did this was out to get me good, maybe even kill me. Just couldn't see who it was. Damn it all to hell! I never closed an eye last night. If I ever come across the person who did this to me, I'm gonna kill him!"

Lew Parker looks at Sam and shakes his head.

"I doubt whether you'll have much success doing it with that hand of yours. I don't think whoever did that, wanted you dead. Whoever it was, had the chance to do it. The way I see and hear it, your attacker wanted to put you out of action and make you suffer, which he or she managed to do."

Sam is in a really foul mood. The sleepless night is starting to take its toll on him. He feels sick to his stomach and his head is spinning. Sam licks his lips.

"Well, what the hell you gonna do about it, Lew? I been maimed for the rest o' my life!"

"Yeah well, Sam, can't say that I blame the one who did this to you. You've been pretty rotten to a lot o' people around here. We'll have to wait an' see how this plays out. If I were you, I'd apologize to everybody I done wrong. That might just save your hide. Since you can't tell me anythin' else, I'll be on my way. Remember; things have a way of comin' back an' bitin' you in the ass, so watch your back!"

Lew opens the door and departs, leaving the door ajar. Sam sits on the bed for a moment, staring at the open door, then he gets up and closes it. He leans against the door, thinking about everything Lew Parker has said to him.

"Damn them all!" he says out loud to himself. "I won't crawl before anybody. Everyone gets what they deserve. They can kiss my ass!"

06H15AM, A FEW MILES outside of Crystal Valley.

Lucy sits astride her mare overlooking the ranch of Sam Cohen from a low hilltop. She came here with one thing foremost in her mind; to make the other ranch hand who was with Sam when her parents were shot, pay for what he'd done.

Lucy doesn't have a plan worked out yet, but she is sure everything will fall into place like it's supposed to. She is a firm believer of fate. Lucy checks the mechanism of her Winchester Carbine and both actions of her six-guns. Satisfied that her firearms are in excellent working order, she starts towards the outbuildings. Riding down the dirt road Lucy pulls her trench coat's hood over her head and places her Stetson on top of it.

Two figures emerge from what has to be the bunkhouse and waits for her to approach. The sun is rising behind Lucy, forcing the two men to cover their eyes partly with cupped hands in order to try to make out who their visitor is. One of them shouts out.

"Hey, who're you an' what you doin' on Sam's ranch? He ain't here by the way; he's in town. Come back when he's here, if it's him you're lookin' to see!"

Lucy halts her mount and stares at them, making the one who had spoken, nervous.

"Take off your hat an' that hood so's I can see your face. Who you lookin' fer, man? Like I said; Sam's in town!"

Lucy speaks for the first time, and the tone of her voice makes them start.

"I know Sam's in town; met with him last night. He isn't feeling too well today, and he's missing a hand. I'm here looking for the man who rode with Sam about two weeks ago and went to the Double Diamond ranch not so far from here ..."

"Who'd you say you was lookin' for, stranger?"

The other ranch hand turns his head, a confused expression on his face.

"Hey, Junior, this stranger was just askin' 'bout you, man! This here's a woman. I just heard her ..."

"Yes; it's you! I recognize your face from that night you came to my parent's ranch and cold-bloodedly gunned them down. It's payback time, Junior! Say a prayer, coz I hope you burn in hell!"

Lucy removes her Stetson, then the trench coat's hood. The men inhale sharply. They can't believe their eyes. Lucy sees the shock that lies shallow in their eyes and she smiles.

"Yes, it's me, Junior; Lucy! Have you said your prayer yet; it's time to say goodbye!"

Junior throws his hands up as Lucy's first bullet smacks into his belly. A second shot sprays half of his brain-matter over the men standing close to him. They run for cover. Lucy turns her horse and bolts. She hears screams behind her.

"Get the horses and stop her! How the hell'd she survive the wound in her back? We have to hurry up, she's goin' to get away!"

Lucy runs her horse approximately one mile before she steers it behind a large boulder and dismounts. She has a good lookout on the trail from here. Lucy doesn't have to wait long before she hears the distant thunder of hooves. She unsheathes her Winchester and levers a round into the chamber; brings the rifle up, sight and eyes lined up in perfect precision.

Her forefinger rests on the trigger as the gang of eight men ascend the slanted trail, lashing their mounts. She waits patiently until five of the eight riders top the slope before she squeezes the trigger. Lucy fires as fast as she can work the lever-action on her rifle. The six men riding in front meet their death without knowing what went wrong or having the opportunity to squeeze off a single shot.

Lucy walks out from behind the boulder and fires a round into the air. The remaining two men halt their mounts, their hands on their gun butts.

Lucy shakes her head.

"Uh-uh, boys; I wouldn't do that if I were you. My trigger finger's still itching."

Lucy looks the two men over. She points her rifle at one of the men.

"You; unbuckle your gun-belt and drop the gun. I'm letting you live because I want you to give Sam a message from me. Do you understand? Nod your head if you do. Alright then; go and tell him I'm alive and well and that I'll be coming for him when I'm good and ready. Got that? Good, you can go."

The ranch hand doesn't wait for a second invitation. He hurriedly turns his horse and speeds off in the direction of town. Lucy indicates with her rifle for the remaining man to dismount.

"You're the other guy who was with Sam the day Logan and I caught you branding his cattle. One of your bullets hit Logan in the chest. You're lucky he isn't dead, because I'm going to give you the chance you never gave him, which is to defend yourself. Just for interest sake; who shot me in the back? I must say that was a very cowardly thing to do."

The man is very pale and stutters when he talks.

"Please, please, miss, I beg you; don't kill me. Sam ordered me to shoot Logan. I would never have done it out of my own free will! I'll disappear, leave the State; just let me go, please."

His pleading sounds so sincere that it makes Lucy drop her guard for a second and look away. Her eye catches a movement as she does so. The man laughs sarcastically as he points the gun at Lucy.

"You give me a chance to defend myself? I think it's gonna be the other way around, missy. Sam shot you the first time around. I admire your shootin', but I ain't Sam. My name's Pedro, and I'll make sure you're dead this time. I'm a better ..."

Lucy moves faster than the blink of an eye. Pedro is still busy talking when he becomes aware of the most intense pain he's ever experienced before he hears the loud bang. He sees the smoking gun in Lucy's hand and looks down, his gun hand faltering. Blood oozes from a large hole in his gut, and Pedro can feel the life flow from his body. He sinks down on his knees and looks up at Lucy.

"I told you I was going to give you a fair chance; you blew it and called the shots."

Pedro's eyes die. He falls forward face in the dirt. There is a last involuntary twitch before he lies dead quiet. Lucy is happy with the way things have turned out. She will deal with Sam later. It's time to head back to town and see how Logan is doing. Vultures are flying overhead; they've come for their pound of flesh.

CHAPTER EIGHT

Lucy finds both Lew and his nightshift Deputy in the Sheriff's office. The surprise on both men's faces when she walks through the door is priceless.

The deputy, Wesley, is the first to respond.

"See; what did I tell you, Lew?"

Lew leans back in his chair.

"Where the hell you been, Lucy? I been lookin' all over town for you! You storm outta Doc Ford's rooms and just disappear. You alright?"

Lucy frowns and nods her head.

"Yes, I'm fine, Lew, but why're you asking? Did I miss something?"

Lew shakes his head.

"Well, for one thing; Sam was attacked and shot last night. He didn't see his attacker or who shot him. His right hand's shot up and Doc says he'll never have use of it again. Do you know something about it, Lucy?"

"Not a thing, Lew. I just came back from our ranch right this minute. I went there yesterday to see if any of the ranch hands are still around. They're still there; fixed the place up some. I slept over in the bunkhouse and came back into town to see how Logan is doing. Is he any better?"

Lew shrugs his shoulders and rises from his chair.

"I don't know, Lucy. I'll walk with you; let's go have us a look. Thanks for helpin' me out this mornin', Wes. You can head on home now. Oh yeah; you can come in at ten tonight. I'll leave the office key with Charlie at the saloon."

Arriving at the Doctor's rooms, they are invited inside. At Lucy's enquiry about Logan's condition, Doc Ford smiles and shows her through to his room. Lew follows a short step behind her. Upon their entrance, Lucy finds it hard not to shout out in surprise.

Logan is in an upright position against the bedpost. Although still weak, the color is back in his face and he smiles at Lucy when she enters the room. Lucy hurries to his bedside, drowning him in kisses. Doctor Ford thinks it wise to put a stop to Lucy's charade.

"Lucy, you don't want Logan to get too excited. He came out of his coma just last night. I removed both bullets with surgery, so he's still a little on the weak side."

"Thank you, Doc. Will you and Lew mind if I spoke to Logan alone for just a couple of minutes?"

Lew and the Doctor excuse themselves and leave the room. Lew returns to the waiting area. Lucy waits until she is sure she and Logan are alone before she leans forward and talks in a subdued voice to Logan.

"I'm going after Sam, but not right now. I know that he killed my parents, and found out that he's the one responsible for shooting both of us. If Lew hadn't come along, we would've died out there. Sam needs to take the punishment to fit the crime."

Logan holds his hand up.

"Leave it to Lew, baby. You're not the Law. Sam murdered your parents in cold blood, and the Law has to take its course here. Just tell Lew what you know, please. I don't wanna lie here and worry about you bein' in danger; it won't do me no good."

Lucy is immovable and shakes her head in denial.

"Logan, it's my parents he killed; I have to be the one to finish this. Please understand. I'm sure you would have felt exactly the same had our roles been reversed. This is one thing I intend to see through, and I won't let anyone stand in my way."

Seeing how adamant Lucy is, Logan knows it won't do him any good to argue with her any longer. He nods his head in defeat.

"Alright, baby, I understand. Just be careful, and watch your back. Where you goin' to do it?"

"I don't know yet; I'll see when the opportunity presents itself. I want it to be a surprise!"

Logan laughs and grabs at his chest.

"Yeow, that hurt! It's goin' to be a surprise, alright. Wish I could be there to see his face. It's rather sad, though. To think everything could've been so different if he only let us help him through that difficult time in his life after his parents died. We were the best of friends once; now we're the worst of enemies."

Lucy is silent for a moment before she reacts.

"Yes, I know. That's why it's so difficult for me. It's going to be gruesome, Logan, but I can't leave it. I'll just hate myself later, and that will destroy me, as well as our relationship. When it's over and done with, we'll be able to carry on with our lives.

Two months later; Sam Cohen's ranch.

The time is 05h45AM. Sam looks in disgust at his hand that has never healed. The hole caused by the bullet, has closed up, but he has no use of it. He can't hold a cup, cut with a knife or hold a gun for that matter. Sam lives like a recluse, and has only one other person besides himself who lives on the ranch. It's a lady who cooks for him and cleans his house.

Sam has been waiting every day, living in anxious anticipation ever since the ranch hand gave him Lucy's message. He can't go to Sheriff Parker with the threat. That'll mean he'd have to tell Lew the truth about his role in the killing of Lucy's parents. He'll probably be hung for murder.

No; he'll much rather take his chances with Lucy. Sam has an arsenal of guns, rifles and ammo stashed everywhere throughout the house, and he constantly watches all directions his house can be approached from. He'll know when Lucy is there before she can surprise him.

LOGAN AND LUCY HAVE been staying on Logan's ranch, the Double-L since Logan became convalesced. He brought Frank with him, who is more than willing to do his share around the ranch. The three of them live in the bunkhouse while Logan and Frank put together the construction of the house. Within a couple of weeks the house is complete.

During this time Lucy keeps their living quarters tidy and cooks their meals. She also does their washing. Logan keeps a watchful eye on Lucy, as she is very quiet and keeps to herself. He hopes she will forget about her vengeance against Sam as time goes by, but he has no way of knowing for sure. Logan decides to just ask Lucy straight-out about it. The opportunity presents itself after dinner one evening. It's just Logan and Lucy in the kitchen; Frank is outside.

"Baby, can I ask you somethin'?"

Lucy has half a smile on her lips when she looks up from where she is pouring them each a mug of coffee.

"You know you can ask me anything you like, Logan. I'll answer it if I can."

"I've been watchin' you now for a while, an' I noticed you were quiet an' withdrawn. Are you still plannin' on goin' after Sam? I promised you that Frank an' I are goin' to rebuild your parent's ranch as soon as we're completely done here."

Lucy sits down opposite Logan.

"That's a question I don't intend answering. I told you it's not necessary to rebuild my parent's ranch. It's mine now, and our land borders onto one another, so let's make it one very large ranch. That way both of our cattle will have more than enough land to roam around free. My horses too!"

Lucy comes around the table and stands against Logan, disheveling his hair. Taking Logan's face between her hands, Lucy bends down and kisses him. Logan sighs and smiles back although he has a very uneasy feeling about Lucy's evasive answer.

xxx

04h00AM; some distance from the Double-L ranch.

A quarter-moon rides low in the pitch black sky. Almost no stars are visible through the dense clouds that warn of an approaching blizzard. Lucy uses the darkness to her fullest advantage, standing tight against a wall of Sam's house close to the back entrance. Lucy left Logan's ranch very early and quietly, making sure not to disturb either of the sleeping men.

Lucy waits patiently for sunrise. She will make her move when the first greyness of dawn appears in the sky. Sam is unaware of her presence, because Lucy saw a light go on about half an hour after her arrival, which means that he was still sleeping when she arrived.

As Lucy stands there, darkness falls away speedily. The first rays of sunlight break through as grey and red break over the horizon simultaneously. The sun reflects off of a shiny object in a window not far from Lucy, and she guesses that it could be Sam standing at the window with a rifle.

Lucy sees the housekeeper open the back door and peer around the doorframe in the direction of the bunkhouse. Lucy waits until the housekeeper pulls her head back before she rams the door open, sending the housekeeper reeling backwards. She bumps her head against the table and slumps down on the floor. There is a shout of alarm.

"Nina, Nina! You alright in there?"

Lucy bides her time. Footsteps come slowly down the corridor, hesitantly. Time stands still for Lucy. Sam comes into view; he sees the housekeeper lying on the floor. His posture becomes rigid; eyes darting nervously around the room. Sam slowly turns around, aware of someone else's presence in the room. His six-shooter comes up when a voice cautions him.

"Rather not, Sam. Toss it."

Sam looks incredulously at the figure facing him. Even ready to kill him, she is still the most beautiful woman he has ever laid eyes on. He's tried during the years since their friendship has failed, to hate her, but he can't. His mouth pulls into a smile.

"Hey there; Lucy. How you doin'? Been waitin' for you to come; even prepared to get you before you could reach my house. Now, here you are, outsmarting me at my own game. I..."

Lucy silences him. She also notices that Sam has changed his image. His hair is shorter and neatly styled, and he has shaved. He looks better.

"Quiet, Sam. I didn't come here to talk. You know the reason why I came here, so cut the small talk and ..."

Sam holds his hand up and Lucy stops talking. His hand looks bad, and she can't help but feel sorry for him.

"Lucy, look, I know why you're here, an' I want you to know that I don't blame you. If I was you, I would've shot me long ago. I would like to say somethin' before you shoot me, though. I had me a lot o' time to think about the past, an' all the things I did an' didn't do. First o' all, I want to say how sorry I am for killin' your parents. I had no reason to do a heinous thing like that, an' I wish I could turn the clock back to that day. Second to all, I'm sorry for pushing you an' Logan away after what my father did. It's my fault our friendship came to an end. An' then, sorry for shootin' you in the back the way I did; it was cowardly. That's it; just wanted to clear my conscience. I been havin' a real hard time sleepin' these past few months."

He holds his mangled hand up.

"The person who done this actually did me a favor, you know? It's what got me thinkin'."

Sam's voice breaks and trails off. A single tear breaks from his eyes and rolls down his cheek. Lucy draws her six-shooter and lifts her arm. The hammer is already cocked. The hair-trigger only needs a very small amount of pressure to set it off. Sam turns his face back towards Lucy.

Lucy sees the raw pain and emotion that lies shallow in Sam's eyes, and try as she may, Lucy can't muster the strength to squeeze the trigger. It suddenly comes to Lucy in a flash. That's the reason why she has kept on extending the standoff with Sam. Lucy's voice is husky with raw emotion when she speaks to Sam.

"Sam, I forgive you. I'm not going to shoot you. Killing you won't make us even. I've done worse things in my life than you, and someone once gave me a second chance to start over. I'm giving you that opportunity now. Take it."

Lucy holsters her gun and turns around.

"See you around, Sam, and help your housekeeper."

Sam lifts his hand in greeting, a smile making his face come alive.

""Thank you, Lucy; see you around."

Lucy walks to where she has left her horse. She mounts her mare and heads for the Double-L ranch at a fast gallop.

86

CHAPTER Nine

Logan sits on the top step of the porch smoking a self-rolled cigarette. He watches Lucy as she enters the gate from the trail. She seems relaxed, riding leisurely. Her hair flows softly in the gentle breeze that is blowing the storm clouds away. It seems like the blizzard has passed over.

Lucy halts her horse and jumps off, smiling at Logan as he rushes to meet her.

They share a passionate kiss before Logan asks.

"You alright? How was the ride; you go anywhere in particular?"

Lucy smiles up at Logan.

"Yes, as a matter of fact, I did. I went to tell Sam that I forgive him. He was first to ask for forgiveness, though. Then I remembered that someone also gave me a second chance at life a long time ago. I was tired of carrying this hate around in me all the time. He's thankful for the second chance he got, and I feel free. I also didn't tell Lew what Sam did; he's going to have to live with his conscience for the rest of his life."

Logan looks Lucy up and down, his glance speaking of worship. Logan points to the pasture.

"Let's go an' have a look at what Frank's doin' down there. I think he's busy puttin' up the biggest corral you've ever seen, an' twelve wild Mustangs that need breaking in. Wanna go an' have a look?"

Lucy flings her arms around Logan's neck and laughs.

"Yes! Let's go and have a look; I can't wait to see the Mustangs!"

Logan and Lucy walk hand in hand in the direction of the new corral, a new chapter in their life just beginning.

The End

About the Author:

Clay Cassidy was born and raised in a small town where the main source of income is mining gold. Clay is famous in the Western genre for his unique writing style. Apart from writing novels, Clay is also a great artist, and busies himself with oil paintings and pencil sketching when he isn't writing; Wildlife being his favorite genre.

Clay also Edits, Proofreads and formats manuscripts for young and aspiring writers as well as famous novelists. Clay also does book cover designing.

Don't miss out!

Visit the website below and you can sign up to receive emails whenever Clay Cassidy publishes a new book. There's no charge and no obligation.

https://books2read.com/r/B-A-IZFIB-ZXIHD

Connecting independent readers to independent writers.

Did you love *Rebel Cowgirl*? Then you should read *A Dozen Lawmen*[1] by Clay Cassidy!

[2]

There's trouble in Gunsight. What the citizens of this Silver - mining town need, is someone to take charge of their problem and sort out the evil forces set on taking over their livelihood. Blake Farraday, a United States Marshall, is that man. Annie Poise contacts him for help. Blake and his Deputies. eleven of them to be exact, arrive in Gunsight and quickly sparks are flying. The towns' Sheriff is on the payroll of an Outlaw bound to become rich from the land he is unlawfully taking from the owners. A small war ensues between the citizens of Gunsight and the Outlaws, led by Blake Farraday and his deputies. The opposing side consisting Rebel Outlaws and hired guns, loose the battle, but Blake loses good men during the battle, too. Was it worth the effort?

---

1. https://books2read.com/u/mBnJYZ

2. https://books2read.com/u/mBnJYZ

Also by Clay Cassidy

Payback
The Judge
The Return
The Serial Killer
A Dozen Lawmen
Wrong Diagnosis
Rebel Cowgirl